HOSPITAL GAMES

HOSPITAL GAMES

Ross McRonald, MD

ReadersMagnet, LLC

Hospital Games
Copyright © 2021 by Ross McRonald, MD

Published in the United States of America
ISBN Paperback: 978-1-955603-87-4
ISBN eBook: 978-1-955603-86-7

The opinions expressed by the author are not necessarily those of ReadersMagnet, LLC.

ReadersMagnet, LLC
10620 Treena Street, Suite 230 I San Diego, California, 92131 USA
1.619.354.2643 I www.readersmagnet.com

Book design copyright © 2021 by ReadersMagnet, LLC. All rights reserved.
Cover design by Ericka Obando
Interior design by Mary Mae Romero

CONTENTS

*This book is dedicated to my friend and lover, my wife, Carole,
for her support and encouragement in all my endeavors.*

INTRODUCTION

This book has taken me almost fifty years to write. I hope the reader understands the reasons. It is 80 percent true. The characters are true, but obviously, the names have been changed. I've taken the liberty of changing some time frames, and in an attempt to make it readable, I have chosen to omit and add certain events. Almost all the characters are dead. It is a difficult time for me, as a physician, but even worse for some of the unfortunate few.

Now after almost a half century, I suspect that many of the same stories are being played out in hospitals around the country. I was struck by the story of a California hospital that allowed a cardiac surgeon to continue operating on healthy people even after the administrator and board were alerted by a number of doctors. The bottom line was just too enticing. I'm certain many other doctors have had similar experiences. The story is also a metaphor on what happens when politics, with a small *p*, interfaces with medicine.

If this book, and Ron Campbell, makes it sound preposterous with all the events, so be it. I'm certain that any number of physicians can relate. I'm either fortunate or unfortunate enough to have a long memory.

If some of the cases seem vaguely familiar, I encourage you to research them. They make for interesting reading.

CHAPTER ONE

He parked his 1978 Mercedes in the doctor's parking lot. It was a year old, but Ron Campbell had owned it for all of two weeks. It was a diesel, and he had purchased it because of the oil crisis. He would have liked a small sports car, but even though his wife had a station wagon, they needed two big cars in the event one needed to go to the shop. Four kids made a carful.

He could have gone in the front door of the hospital, but the ER door was just as close. And besides, he wanted to catch up on any news or gossip. Dr. Campbell was just thirty-five, and although he was a touch less than six feet, he seemed taller to most people. It was due to his slender frame and military-type bearing. It was a remainder from his time a few years earlier as a naval medical officer.

The ER was small. The entire hospital was small, just 120 beds. It had opened six years earlier, and Campbell was an initial staff member. In the navy, he would have been called a plank owner. When the hospital had opened, he and two other doctors had set up the emergency room medical staff.

Campbell and a number of other staff doctors initially rotated through the shifts manning the ER twenty-four hours a day. Now there was one full-time doctor working the midnight shift, and they were advertising for more full-time staff. The full-timer wasn't very good but was the only one who had applied for the job. For the new doctors in practice, it added some income. Some were family doctors and internists, and three were surgeons. Emergency room physicians hadn't been invented yet.

The ER was almost empty with only one cubicle occupied. He saw Dottie Roots, the charge nurse, quickly beckon to him from behind the work station.

"Morning, Dot. What's up?"

She replied with her forefinger, signaling him to lean over. "Did you hear?"

"What?" Ron obviously wasn't privy to the news.

"They shipped a kid out last night with asthma to Oceanside, and she died on the way."

Ron thought he saw her start to cry. "How old?" An irrelevant comment, but it was something to say.

"Twelve. Her name was Millhouse."

"Millhouse! I have patients by that name. Oh god, I hope it's not the same family." It might not be, but in the small town where Fairtown Hospital was located, it probably was. It was an unusual name. "What happened?"

"As I got the story, she came in around eleven, and they tried to stabilize her. But she was still in status, and they sent her to the floor anyway." Status asthmaticus is critical. "They called her pediatrician three or four times, but he never came in. He told them to send her to Oceanside." There was no house staff at Fairtown. Bill Williams, the hospital administrator, had repeatedly told the medical staff that he couldn't afford house staff.

"Who's her doctor?" He used the present tense. "Hernandez." Her expression said it all.

Mario Hernandez was chief of pediatrics and the recently elected chief of staff.

Ron almost reeled. It had happened again. He knew it would.

Ron Campbell was the clinical director of a family practice residency based at Oceanside. The director was a semiretired pediatrician. Campbell was one of only two board-certified family doctors in the area. He split his time between his practice and teaching residents. It was a hectic routine, but he felt it was worth it. He kept up with new developments, and the residents were constantly challenging him, making for interesting medicine.

Six months before this untimely death, he had walked into a buzz saw at Oceanside. John Sailor, his chief, along with Ned Zowicki, the chief of pediatrics and his own kids' doc, along with Chris Thomas, the chief of medicine, were ensconced in Sailor's office.

"What happened in that shithole hospital of yours?" Ned said it with a smile.

Ron was taken aback. "No idea. I haven't been to the hospital yet." "Well, last night, about three, we got an asthmatic shipped over from

your place. Had a pCO_2 of almost 140 and no endotracheal tube." He was saying that the amount of carbon dioxide was almost fatal. An endotracheal tube would at least have helped.

"Who was his doctor?" Ron just assumed the patient was a boy. "Your buddy, Hernandez." Ned smirked at him. He knew Ron disliked

the man.

"Is the kid okay?"

"Yeah, we broke his attack, and now he's breathing without a tube. He can probably go home tomorrow."

Ron was still standing with his coat on. He stripped off the jacket, collecting his thoughts. They were waiting for him to say something. Finally, he opened up. "Why don't you guys write a letter to the administrator, the medical staff, or the board of trustees? Tell them what happened?"

"Why us? It's your problem," Sailor asked.

"Because you all know what is happening there. They won't give me the time of day. Not at their precious hospital." Ron was alluding to the board of trustees or, more appropriately, the executive body of the board, most of whom were business owners in town and were getting contracts from the hospital.

Ron was disgusted with the answer. He turned and went to his desk and picked up his mail. Saying anything more would only incense him, and he was afraid of what he would say. A child had almost died, and they didn't care.

CHAPTER TWO

From the time Fairtown opened in 1972, it had struggled. The hospital had been conceived about seven years earlier. It was the brainchild of a few businesspeople in the town. It was twenty miles from any other hospital in the state. In the nineteen thirties, a general practitioner had opened a ten-bed "hospital" in his large home on Main Street. It literally was his hospital. But he was intelligent enough to see the handwriting on the wall and attempted to get the few other doctors in town to enlarge it and make it a more inclusive facility. Who knew what really happened, but prior to the Second World War, the hospital closed when the doctor died. The town became fallow ground as far as a hospital was concerned.

Fairtown was old with a revolutionary history. The town had a traditional Main Street, a microcosm of what Americans remembered. Anchoring the middle of town was the old county courthouse that was the site of a famous murder trial involving a doctor accused of killing his wife. He was defended by a famous attorney. The doctor lost and went to jail. Two pharmacies faced each other on opposite corners. There was a hotel said to be dated from the late seventeen hundreds with a restaurant and bar, along with a restaurant advertising Tomato Pies above the door. Some buildings had cornerstones dating to the mid-eighteen hundreds. An old GP told Ron that he remembered, as a boy, driving cattle down Main Street when most of it was dirt.

One small modern building on the edge of town housed a new medical laboratory. Sitting on the windowsill of the director's office was a large jar containing half of a human brain. The director, Dr. Harvey, was quick to identify it as Albert Einstein's. It became the basis of a book many years later called *Driving Mr. Albert.* Interspersed along Main Street were offices of the town's older physicians—mostly general practitioners, no surgeons or other specialists. The town was also backdrop for a young man who would become one of the world's best-known rock stars, basing many of his lyrics on his hometown.

It was a community that was set in its ways and not prepared for the influx of young commuters moving out from the city and the malls that would follow. When Fairtown Hospital opened, the same attitude that was prevalent in the nineteen thirties seemed to permeate the new institution. There was no cooperation between the new, young physicians and those who had been in town for twenty or thirty years. There was immediate tension. The initial board of trustees was made up of businessmen without any medical experience. Most had a vested interest in how the hospital could benefit them. Although they professed that the reason for the hospital was for the community, it really was a cash cow. Money was readily available from the federal government for new health-care construction. They hired an administrator and moved to recruit a medical staff without which they couldn't fill the beds. The administrator was about forty and hadn't run a hospital prior to this. The board of trustees, new to hospital workings, was happy to have a malleable administrator.

The first thing that the administrator needed for the medical staff was a radiologist and an anesthesiologist. George Steinshaft was an anesthesiologist, and the radiologist Tom Consenti was from the state capital thirty miles west. Neither was accredited by physicians, both being the sole choice of the new administrator. It was soon evident that neither had been screened by physicians. A few years later when Campbell asked to see their résumés, Williams told him that he didn't have the authorization. The hospital opened without a cardiologist, pulmonologist, full-time orthopedist, and only one board-certified internist and one board-certified family physician, Ron Campbell. The remainder was a mélange of older GPs. Many of the new doctors applying to the staff were foreign trained. Some were excellent, but others not so well—the same as the rest of the staff. But in that era, it resulted in degrees of distrust and, at times, discrimination.

Complicated cases frequently fell through the cracks when those were cared for by unqualified doctors without any consultants available. That, mixed with the burgeoning young population of people who had been accustomed to medical care in the city, caused distrust in the hospital.

As was true of many hospitals, the surgeons liked to take charge. They utilized the facility more than anyone. Fairtown was no different. Carl Riggs had settled in Fairtown a couple of years before the hospital opened. There was a rumor that he had his privileges curtailed at another hospital, but that was never documented. The rumor persisted because Riggs wasn't a very good surgeon. But he was the supreme deal maker and schmoozer. Many loved his bedside manner. It was a blow to him when a hometown boy, Stephen English, left a teaching hospital in Philadelphia to open an office. English wanted to chair the surgical department and felt that, with his credentials, he should be the one. Riggs had other ideas, and soon the game was on. It would involve life and death.

Just prior to opening the hospital, all of about thirty doctors met to elect the medical executive committee. Riggs became chief of surgery and then was elected chief of staff. Mario Hernandez was named chief of pediatrics. He was the only board-certified pediatrician on the staff. Ken Poorman, an older local doc, was elected chief of family practice. Ron was not selected to be on the board.

When it opened for business, there was an obstetrics wing, ten pediatric beds, and one forty-bed ward. There was a five-bed ICU that doubled as a surgical ICU. Slowly the beds filled, and then they opened the other forty-bed wing. Everyone was new and green. Mistakes happened, but nothing too horrendous.

The growing pains hit the administration. Less than a year into operations, the administrator and chief financial officer were fired. All the medical staff was told was that they "had a problem with billing" and that the hospital had "lost" two or three million dollars. Ron wondered if the loss had been something else. Bill Williams was named the new administrator. It was strange that he was picked as he didn't have the credentials to be a hospital administrator.

Small not-for-profit hospitals were a strange breed. Frequently, they were the largest employer in town—overseen by volunteers and the board of trustees and run by an administrator. No one had any skin in the game. No one took a loss or made a profit. They could be rife with patronage and conflicts of interest. Fairtown was not an exception.

The area around Fairtown was growing rapidly. The original doctors surrounding the hospital's reach were only ten to fifteen, and they tended to be older, some on the cusp of retirement. But the realization that there would be a new hospital had attracted a number of new doctors to the area, many of whom were foreign trained. It created an unfortunate consequence. The staff quickly divided into two camps—those US trained and those not. It was based on the assumption of differences in quality of care.

Campbell had originally planned to be a surgeon, having functioned as one for two years in the navy. He had a surgical residency lined up at a prestigious university, but with three children already, he felt that being thirty- five when he finished his training was too old. He needed to start in practice. The specialty of family practice had just started, and he submitted his credentials and was accepted to take the examination to become board certified. When he passed the exam, he looked for an office. He found a small space that would do initially. He ordered equipment and signed a lease.

He hoped that the practice would grow quickly enough to pay the bills.

Just prior to opening his office, he was in work clothes, attaching wall mounts in his office. He turned around to find his real estate agent and landlord, Jack Ilson, standing behind him.

"Ron, I thought you'd like to meet Dr. Steven English. He just bought a house in town and is going to be a surgeon at Fairtown."

Ron wiped his hands on a towel and put out his hand. "Ron Campbell." It would be the start of a long friendship.

"Steve," he answered. "I understand that you're just out of the navy and are a family doc." Ilson knew Ron's story and, apparently, had briefed him. "Yeah, I'm trying to get this office set up so I can open next week. But in the meantime, I have to hustle up some other work while I try to get the practice off the ground."

English reached into his pants and pulled out a leather wallet. He searched a compartment and gave a card to Campbell. "Call this guy. He runs the ER group at Oceanside. They are looking for staff part-time. I just got a couple of shifts."

Ron took the proffered card. "Thanks, I appreciate that." He looked into a drawer and found a newly printed business card, took out a pen, and wrote his home telephone on the back. "Give me a call. We can get the wives together and have a drink or go out for dinner."

English put the card back into his wallet. "I'd like to reciprocate, but I haven't had cards printed. I'm still looking for office space. Jack is looking around, but the office space is limited."

"Wait until the hospital is finished. There will be more offices opening than doctors to fill them." Ilson was being prophetic. "Well, let's get out of here so that the good doctor can finish up and open on Monday."

They all said their goodbyes, and Ron was left alone to finish his chores.

Ron got home at about six and, after washing up, told Barbara about his meeting with English.

"What's he like?"

"Seems decent enough." It was a cryptic remark. "Well, what does he look like?"

"About my height and slender. Has a 'stache and big sideburns. Typical seventies look." Ron still favored close-cropped hair and was clean-shaven. A holdover from his navy days, but one that would not leave him. "He gave me a contact for some ER work at Oceanside. I thought that was nice of him."

"He should be nice to you."

"Why?" Ron was puzzled by the remark.

"Heh, stupid. He's a surgeon. Where do you think he'll get cases?

From you." She was grinning at him.

Ron was so wrapped up in getting the office open and looking for work he had never grasped the implications in the meeting. Life lessons were being learned.

Ron had known Barbara since grammar school, where they had been in the same classroom for six years. She lived around the corner from him but, in high school, had dated older guys. She was always too thin for him. That all changed when she showed up at the local college they had both transferred to. She was stunning, blond, and beautifully dressed. He fell in love instantly and pursued her relentlessly, shooing away all the guys who were interested. They married just after graduation and then went to Upstate New York to medical school. They had their first child in his senior year when she stopped working and he joined the navy.

He had first done an internship in the naval hospital in Philadelphia. Prior to graduation, his internship class was given the duty stations that were available. Flight surgeon, submarine medicine, or fleet marines— essentially a thirteen-month tour in Vietnam. The war was heating up. Ron initially selected flight surgeon but was told in no uncertain terms that he wouldn't be accepted because he was color-blind. He almost panicked when he asked about sub school. They would give him a waiver. With two young children, he didn't want to be away for over a year. Doctors weren't getting killed in Vietnam. Submarines went to sea for three months at a time. After sub school, he was scheduled for two patrols.

The following day Ron called Oceanside, got an interview that afternoon, and within an hour, had one twelve-hour shift in their ER starting at six in the evening and ending at six in the morning. It would help pay the bills. When he got home, Barbara told him that Lenore English had called, introduced herself, and invited them for drinks and to go to the Continental for dinner that Saturday.

"Did you accept?"

"I tentatively said yes, pending that you didn't have anything else. I told her that I would get back to her after I talked to you to confirm and get directions. Who do you think is buying? They invited us."

"We're going to split it. I don't want to be indebted. But let's see what happens." Ron had a strict moral code.

They called the four kids, and then they all sat down to dinner. Along with breakfast, it was the only time the family got together.

Three nights later, Ron and Barbara drove across town to a new development. They found English's house and were greeted by both Steve and Lenore at the door. Their home was new and only sparsely furnished. They found their way into the kitchen.

"Drink, anyone?" Steve asked.

"White wine, if you have it," Barbara replied.

Steve nodded at Lenore. "You too?" She nodded in affirmation. "Ron, what will you have?"

"Scotch. On the rocks," he added.

"Good, that's my poison too." English took out glasses and poured very generous portions. "What shall we toast?"

"How about to a successful opening of the hospital?" Barbara opined. "How about 'to successful practices'? To hell with the hospital. We all have to eat," Steve said it with a laugh. Ron felt like it was an auspicious start.

After a half hour of feeling-out questions—where did you go for med school, where did you train, and family background—Steve offered a second round. Everyone declined, and they took Steve's Lincoln to the Continental restaurant. Ron and Barb had passed it a number of times but had never eaten there. The food was just okay. But the drinks were large, and there was music. At ten they left and got back to Steve's home.

"Nightcap?"

Ron looked at Barbara for commitment, and she nodded. "Just one.

We have a babysitter."

That one wound up at three during which time Ron and Steve recognized that their medical philosophies were almost identical. They practiced ethical medicine, and anything less was not acceptable. They also found someone who they could drink with and laugh.

CHAPTER THREE

Campbell had moved into the town just east of Fairtown. He had been drawn to it since first seeing it while on duty in the navy. It was considered upscale. It was open country and didn't have any doctors. It was the type of town that he and Barbara were seeking to raise their children. Fairtown would be the hospital that he would join. Ron initially didn't think he was "of" Fairtown, but since he admitted his patients there, along with the parties, fund-raising affairs, and galas that involved Barbara, he became tied to the town. Many of his patients lived in Fairtown.

As the months went by, Campbell's practice built up. Not as fast as he would have liked, but it was attracting the type of patients he enjoyed seeing. They were intelligent and liked the way he discussed their problems. Sorting through the mundane earaches, back problems, and respiratory infections that were the routine in family practice, he even made a few diagnoses that made him proud, like with a parathyroid adenoma patient who, after English had operated, had all her symptoms resolved.

He and English began to talk by phone almost every day. The conversations were often directed at the humorous daily incidents that occur in medicine, but more often, the discussion centered on the type of medicine they were beginning to see at Fairtown. It was not pretty.

After the first year of operation at Fairtown, it was time to vote for new department chiefs and the six at-large seats on the medical executive committee. Ron already knew that he wouldn't be chief of the family medicine department. He sensed, or knew, that his outspoken comments about quality of care made him a threat to some of the other staff. Instead, he tried a bit to be a better politician and gather enough votes to be an at-large member. It would, he hoped, give him a bit more leverage to address some of the needs of the hospital medical staff. By a slim margin, he was elected to the committee.

The first meeting of the newly elected medical executive committee was contentious even though the only agenda items were election of officers and naming committee heads. English had worked a coup himself and had defeated Riggs for the chief of surgery. The makeup of the board now seemed ideal for a try at chief of staff. After a few word from both Riggs, the present chief hoping for another term, and English, a secret ballot was polled. Steven English became the new chief of staff. Ron was named chairman of the ICU Committee. Ron thought that this would be the beginning of the new era. It was to be but not the way he had envisioned. The chief of staff, English, was thirty-six, and the average age of the board was somewhere around the same age. Bill Williams, the hospital administrator, in his first comment after the election, was a bit of a slap at the members. "I wish that we had a few more grayheads" was his snide comment that he didn't like all these young firebrands running the show. Williams was a holier-than-thou type and wore his religion on his sleeve. Although he was not vocal, one could sense that he had difficulty with the staff because of a predominance of Jewish physicians. His conflicts with English and then, indirectly, with Campbell were apparent from the start. The staff polarization began to widen. It wasn't apparent to Campbell at that time, but he came to realize that Williams was going to utilize those differences to his own advantage. He had to protect his turf.

Ron didn't realize it until a couple of years later when a young assistant vice president pointed out that he had better credentials than Williams. Williams didn't have a master's degree.

The month after the election, Ron spent the little free time he had going over protocols of the ICU with Ann Ciardi. It seemed strange that here he was a young family doc running the ICU. But it was a reflection of the staff. Perhaps one or two others in the internal medicine department could have done it, but they didn't want to be bothered. There wasn't a cardiologist or pulmonologist on staff. He was also on the phone once or twice a day with English, developing an agenda for the up-and-coming med exec meeting.

It was five thirty in the afternoon, and Ron was finishing his charts and making callbacks. His telephone buzzed, and Patti, his receptionist/ assistant, informed him that Dr. English was on the line.

"High, Steve. What's up?"

"Ron, we now have six surgeons on staff. A urologist and an orthopod are joining. We also have two eye guys, and the OB department is pushing two hundred deliveries a year. We only have Steinshaft as an anesthesiologist. He basically lives at the hospital and runs from room to room. I don't think it's safe and want to bring it up at the meeting."

"Okay, I agree, but what are you really trying to tell me?"

"Steinshaft is crazy." English tended to exaggerate, but Ron had found Steinshaft more than a bit odd. "Besides that he never stays with the patient even if I'm deep into a case. He runs out to give OB anesthesia or whatever. Yesterday I was doing a colon resection, and the blood looked too dark. I peeked over the screen at the pulse ox, and it was 86 percent. George wasn't around. I had to have him paged. It could have been a disaster. When he showed up, he was pissed that I called him.

"I want to push for another gas passer."

"How do you think Crazy George is going to take it?"

"I could care less. We've got to move this hospital forward. Right now it's just a pissant place."

"Well, I'll support it. Do you think you should run it by Williams first?"

"Maybe, if the time is right and I see him in the hospital. I don't want to do it over the phone. He frequently puts you on speaker, and you don't know who's in the room with him. I just wanted to run it by you. Now I'm going to call Bob and see what he says." English terminated the call.

Bob Garth was the chief of obstetrics. He was levelheaded but seemed to work diligently to stay out of the politics. But this was important to his department.

Ron didn't give the plan much of a thought. It wouldn't cost the hospital. Anesthesiologists billed separately. But it would cut into Steinshaft's income considerably. But Steve was right. It just wasn't appropriate to have one gas passer.

The rest of the week went quickly, and on Thursday evening, Ron ate a quick dinner at home and went back to the hospital. He checked a couple of sick patients before heading to the boardroom, where the med exec committee met. He found a seat and then headed to the coffee maker for a cup of black coffee. It could be a long night. He read over the one- page agenda that was on the table in front of every chair. It was pretty standardized— Minutes, Old Business—but under New Business, the first item was simply labeled *anesthesia*. It seemed innocuous. It wasn't.

The medical executive board was composed of eight department heads: pathology, radiology, anesthesia, pediatrics, internal medicine, obstetrics/ gynecology, family practice, and surgery. There were six at-large members and Bill Williams, the administrator.

After calling the meeting to order, English quickly dispensed with initial basic items and then moved to New Business.

"I want to bring up the question of why we only have one anesthesiologist. Between general surgery, ophthalmology, gyn, and urology, we're running two ORs constantly. That doesn't include delivery. Any comments?"

"Steven." It came out with a wheeze. "There aren't enough cases to support two anesthesiologists. No one wants to come here." Steinshaft was making his case.

"What do you mean 'nobody wants to come here'? Have any docs applied?" English was surprised at the comment. "Bill?" He was directing the question to the administrator.

"Well, three people have inquired. None submitted an application. I talked to them and told them to make an appointment with George before they go through the paperwork. Two showed up."

"And?"

Williams shrugged his shoulders. "None followed up."

"Did you talk to them after they had interviewed with George?"

"No, they just left."

Steve quickly eyed Ron. They both suspected the same thing. Steinshaft had chased them away.

English thought quickly. "Why don't we put together a committee to do the next interview? Bob"—nodding at Garth— "why don't you chair it? Pick who you want."

"Steve, I don't have the time. We're looking for a third guy and are too busy."

Riggs finally spoke up. He appeared to be having a bad day. When things were difficult, it seemed that his bald head started to flake. It was now. He spoke in a quiet tone, "Steve, why are you jumping at this? George is doing a terrific job. Let him handle it. I'm certain that someone will come along."

"Carl, you know we need someone else. George is driving them away." English was showing some irritation.

The gauntlet had been thrown down. It took some months before Ron realized that this was a turning point in the hospital. Political sides were hardening, and Williams was happy to see the doctors fighting. They wouldn't be pointing fingers at him.

Ron finally got home at around eleven. Barbara was already in bed but was watching Johnny Carson on the TV.

"So what happened?"

"Not much, but Steve brought up the Steinshaft situation."

"And?" She was prompting him to go on.

"Nothing specific at the meeting, but Steve told me that he was going to speak to Bill about any new applicants. He wants to talk to them prior to George. Steinshaft seems to be driving away applicants."

"What did Riggs have to say?"

"What brought that up? You think he knows something?"

"Ronald." It was almost sarcastic. "Riggs hates Steve. Moving into Fairtown has cut into not only his livelihood but his prestige. Losing the chief of staff position was enormous. You two"—she was referring to Steve and himself—"have made yourselves his enemies. He's an easy read. He's uncouth and a bore."

Soon after opening his office, Riggs and his wife, Gerta, had invited the two out for dinner at a country club restaurant. It had been embarrassing. Early on, Riggs attempted to get the waiter's attention by raising his hand, snapping his fingers, and loudly calling Gaston. Ron felt like crawling under the table. It went downhill from there. When the time came to pay the check, Riggs flatly refused to accept the Campbells' half. It went against Ron's ethics.

"So why do you think he was for Steinshaft?"

"Because English is against him. Remember *The Godfather*? When the gangster says something about business and not personal? Well, here it's just the opposite. To Riggs, this is personal. He'll try all sorts of things to get even."

The comment stunned Ron. He was not used to this type of politics.

But Barbara, the daughter of a mayor, had seen her share. "What do you think I should do?"

"Just be careful and keep your big mouth closed." She smiled and turned off the TV. "Go to bed. You have to get up in six hours. Good night." She blew him a kiss and rolled over.

CHAPTER FOUR

It was St. Patrick's Day, but Ron was in his office, seeing patients. Every new patient was a bonus. He had seen one patient refer a couple of others. He had run into Carl Riggs at morning rounds, and he was headed home to be with his kids. They went to a parochial school and had the day off. He lived about forty minutes from the hospital. Ron told him to have fun. At around three in the afternoon, a pharmacist from Fairtown, Ted Edmunds, brought his nine-year-old daughter with a bellyache into the office. Ron examined her carefully and thought she might be having appendicitis.

"I'd be happier if you'd get a surgeon to check her out. It might not be appendicitis, but I'd like to be certain. That way if she gets worse, you have someone to call. I know that Dr. English is in his office now."

"What about Carl Riggs?" Ted Edmunds asked.

"He's okay, but he's at home with his kids," Campbell absentmindedly said while writing in the chart. "Do you want me to call Dr. English?"

"No, thanks, I have his number. But thanks." "Hope everything works out."

At five thirty, as Ron was about to leave the office, the telephone rang.

Patti had already left, and he answered, "Dr. Campbell."

"Ron?" Campbell immediately recognized the smarmy tone of Bob Riggs.

"Oh, hi, Bob. What's up?"

"Why did you send Ted Edmunds to English?" His voice had changed and was angry. "They are longtime patients of mine. You didn't even ask."

Ron was taken aback by the tone and attitude. He had tried to do Riggs a favor and not disturb him. Before he could respond, Riggs continued,

"After all I did for you? I introduced you to people and even sent you a couple of patients."

Ron attempted to keep his cool. "Bob, when I saw you this morning, you were going home to see your kids. I tried to do you a favor and not bother you. Steve was in his office. You're forty minutes away."

"Don't do me any favors. If I find that you send any more of my patients to English, I'll get you." The call was terminated.

Campbell just stared at the phone, dumbstruck. Then he got pissed. *Sonnavabitch, I tried to be nice, and he had the audacity to threaten me. That is the last time I'll ever send him a case.*

Ron reflected back a month or so when Riggs had invited him into the OR to see a colon resection on one of Campbell's patients. Ron couldn't scrub in as an assistant because the hospital had a rule that only surgeons could be at the table. Ron had two years of surgical training in the navy. He had run two so-called dirty surgery wards at the naval hospital. That included a proctology clinic twice a week doing as many as six or seven sigmoidoscopes a day.

On this case, Riggs was going to sigmoidoscope the patient in the OR prior to surgery. Campbell was appalled—a sterile area, and he was going to stick a scope up the patient's rectum. But that wasn't all. He went to pontificate to Ron how to do a sigmoid exam. Ron didn't want to offend since he had probably done more than Riggs and quietly told him he knew how. Riggs never had the courtesy to inquire about his background. Campbell had left the OR prior to the surgery.

It took him a few minutes to cool off, and then he went home.

"How was the office?" Barbara said while she was cooking the obligatory corned beef. The aroma of cooked cabbage was in the house.

Ron went to the cabinet and took out a rocks glass. "You want one?" He was obviously alluding to a drink.

"Yes, please. Make it light."

"Martini?"

"Fine."

"To answer your question, it was fine until just before I left and got a call from Riggs."

"Oh, and what was that about?'

While he mixed the martinis, he reiterated the telephone call. When he finished, Barbara simply said, "Boy, those two must really hate each other." She was referring to English and Riggs. "You really would have hated being a surgeon if that was the kind of crap you had to put up with." Ron handed her the drink. "I was thinking the same thing coming home.

But I was referring a few cases to Riggs even though I suspected he wasn't anywhere as skilled as Steve. Steve told me, but I'd seen it myself, that Riggs operates from the wrong side of the table. But that phone call clinches it. I suspect that I made a real enemy today." He took a long pull on his martini. "I don't know what he can do to me, but I'd better take your advice and be careful. Is that corned beef done?"

Six weeks later at seven fifteen in the morning, Ron heard "code blue ICU" over the hospital paging system. He left the chart he was reading on the nurse's station and quickly got to the ICU. He saw a nurse doing chest compression on an elderly man in bed 3. The curtains were drawn around the other beds. Ann Ciardi was pushing the crash cart to the bedside. Ron glanced at the monitor and the ventricular fibrillation. He got to the bedside, asking, "What's the diagnosis?" He was referring to why the gentleman was in the ICU.

"Came in early this morning by ambulance with abdominal pain. He's Samson's patient. He's eighty-four. Hasn't seen him yet but ordered labs. They were drawn about an hour ago. EKG showed an old infarct. Labs not back yet." Ann summarized the case quickly. Right now they needed to shock the patient and get him out of V-fib.

"Call the lab, and get those results now!" Ron yelled over to the unit secretary. He was setting the defibrillator when George Steinshaft came racing into the unit. He wore a long white laboratory coat and was taking a large syringe from his pocket. It was already full of some medication. He grabbed the IV line and did a quick swipe on the port. He plunged the needle in before Ron could open his mouth. "George, what the hell are you giving him?"

"He's potassium depleted. I'm giving him potassium." "How the hell do you know? The labs aren't back yet." "He's in V-fib. He must be." He withdrew the syringe.

"Stand back," Ron warned the team. He pressed the paddles to the bare chest and pressed the red button. The shock caused the patient to jump involuntarily. Ron glanced up at the monitor. He was still in fibrillation.

Amazingly, Steinshaft pulled out another smaller-loaded syringe. He pushed that into the IV and emptied the syringe. Ron stared at Ciardi, dumbstruck. He asked the obvious, "Doctor, what was that?"

"Calcium."

Ron was too busy with the defibrillator to question him again. The second shock did not change the cardiac outcome. He was upset that he had not been successful. "One more thing. Give me epi and a cardiac needle." He would try to inject directly into the heart. Ann drew up   the medication and gave him the syringe with the six-inch needle. He swiped the chest with alcohol and plunged the needle directly through the chest between the ribs. He withdrew the plunger, slightly seeing dark-red blood flowed back. He was in the heart. He pushed the plunger, and the epinephrine went into the heart.

No change was registered on the monitor. "One more." He was referring to another cardiac shock. He went through the routine again, but nothing changed.

"Doctor, these are the labs." She handed him a printout. "Hemoglobin 7.2, white count 12K. Liver enzymes are off the wall."

"Did Samson get a surgeon to see him?" "Not yet."

"So we admit a patient to the ICU and nobody saw him? What about the ER doc?" Fairtown didn't have a floor doctor.

"They drew the labs in the ER but sent him upstairs because Samson said he would see him on rounds this morning."

"Great. Just great." Ron shook his head. "I'm calling the code." He checked his watch. It was fourteen minutes since he arrived. Not long but with the labs and the three cardiac shocks, he just thought it futile. He had to wonder what the patient's mental status would be like if his heart had reverted to normal rhythm.

He sat down behind the desk and filled in the chart. "Ann, did George tell you how much of that crap he gave the patient?"

She shook her head. "You know he does that all the time. He seems to carry those syringes full with him."

"You're here when all the codes come in the ICU. Does he always use that stuff?"

"Most of the codes."

"Have you seen anyone come out of a code?" "No."

Her reply said it all. "Where do we take this?"

"You tell me. I'm just a charge nurse. You are the head of the ICU."

Campbell felt trapped. The executive board was becoming more and more divided. Quality of care was subverted to politics. It was Riggs against English. How was a family doctor going to go against an anesthesiologist who had the backing of powerful people? Campbell suddenly realized that Riggs and Williams had formed a pact. They had enlisted most of the foreign-trained doctors against them. Steinshaft was being used as the foil. Anything that English wanted, in terms of quality of care, went against the Riggs/Williams group.

CHAPTER FIVE

It just seemed unfortunate at the time, a bad outcome for sick patients. Ron had been working as a doctor for a free clinic, seeing patients for the county health clinic in poor areas. He was paid a minimum stipend, but it helped the down-and-out. The nurse who ran the clinic was a devoted health worker, who rousted out the poor and unwilling to bring their children to the clinic for checkups and immunizations. Some lived in old school buses, some in tar paper shacks. You could see the skyscrapers of New York from some of their homes. He saw a child of two parents—both with college educations—that, at six months, weighed nine pounds. She was living in the bottom drawer of a chest of drawers.

Nora Cheerman, the lead nurse, was a dedicated worker committed to her patients or, as they were beginning to be called, clients.

"Ron." They didn't stand on formalities. "I'm having abdominal pains after I eat. It's pretty intense."

"Worse with fatty foods?" he asked. "Yeah, pizza and bacon are killers." "Go to your back and shoulder?" "How did you know?"

"Nora, it's classic gallbladder disease. Anyone in your family have gallbladder problems?"

"Sure, now that you mention it. My sister and grandmother."

"Nora, you need a GB ultrasound. I'll give you a script so you can get one."

"Where do I go to have it done?"

He explained that there were two places, but he didn't care where she went. He forgot about the conversation.

Two weeks later, while there was a lull in the clinic, she pulled him aside. "What do you think about this?" She pushed a radiology report toward him. He took it and went right to the bottom, the summary.

"Multiple small stones, none in the bile ducts." It confirmed his diagnosis. "Unfortunately, you need surgery." Laparoscopy hadn't been developed.

"Who do you recommend?"

"Nora, Steve English is a superb surgeon when it comes to gallbladder surgery. He can take out your gall with a three-inch incision in thirty minutes. I've seen it done. Give him a call. It doesn't need to be done today. Get it done at your convenience. It goes better that way."

Two weeks later, she told Ron that it was being done on a Friday, four weeks from that day.

Steve called Ron at eleven the morning of the surgery. He always confirmed his surgery with Ron. "I did Nora Cheerman just now. She had a pretty inflamed gallbladder, but it was straightforward. She did well."

"Thanks for the call. Did you tell her kids?" She was divorced and had twin daughters almost eighteen.

"Yeah, they were there with her mother. Everyone went home. By the way, do you know that we're supposed to take in a movie tonight? The girls made plans."

"I suppose. I'll probably fall asleep. I'm beat. I'm going to take my own car. I may bug out early. Just tell me where we're going and when to be there."

Steve told him the theater and the time. He said they would meet there.

The movie wasn't great, and Ron was half asleep when Steve's beeper went off. He quickly silenced it in the theater and went to the pay phone. Three minutes later, he was back at the seats, leaning across the aisle, "Nora Cheerman just coded. I've got to go back."

"Want me to go with you?" Ron asked.

"No, there's nothing that you can do that I can't. Just take the girls home. I'll see you when." He ran out of the theater.

The three sat there for the ending. Ron wasn't interested. He didn't know if the girls were. Ron drove Lenore back to her house. She invited them for a drink. Ron wasn't really interested but wanted to hear what Steve had to say when he got back.

About forty minutes later, Steve pulled in. He was shaken. He grabbed a quick scotch.

Ron was the first to speak. "And?"

"She died. Forty-two. From a routine gallbladder. How the hell did that happen?"

"Who was there?" Ron was asking about the code. "Just George. He said he couldn't revive her."

"Did you get a post?" Ron was concerned about the cause. He was asking about a postmortem.

"Didn't ask. Was too upset. Looking at those two beautiful kids who just lost their mother to a simple operation."

Ron finished his drink. There wasn't anything else to say. "C'mon, Barb, I've got hours tomorrow."

It was Saturday, but Ron was still trying to build his practice. They left Steve. He was agonizing about his lost patient.

On the ten-minute ride home, Ron didn't say anything. When he got home, he poured another drink.

"Another?" Barb asked.

"Sorry, I really liked that woman. She worked to help a lot of piss-poor people. She didn't need to die."

"What do you think happened?"

"Who knows?" He didn't want to say what he really thought—a Friday night, nobody around, and Steinshaft was the one on the code. All this just after English was trying, as the Chinese say, "to break his rice bowl." "Let's go to bed. I have a tough time tomorrow."

CHAPTER SIX

It was a new time for Fairtown. They were going to open the new wing. It would expand med/surg to a hundred beds. Whoopee, the big time. It was staffed with a combination of newly trained nurses, along with older nurses, many having just returned to clinical service. Two days after admitting his first patients to Two West, the new wing, he visited one of his patients. The patient was groggy and almost incoherent. He reviewed the medication chart and found out that the nurse had given the patient ten times the ordered prescription. She had misplaced the decimal point. Ron reacted inappropriately. He screamed at the nurse, "What the hell did you do? You almost killed him!" It was in front of other nurses and a few visiting families. He knew he was wrong as soon as he did it. But no excuses, he'd been up almost all night in the ICU and was scheduled back in his office for eight hours of patients in just thirty minutes. He stormed off the floor.

Just before closing the office, he got a call from Riggs. He was in no mood. "Yeah, what do you want?"

"Dr. Campbell?" Ron was puzzled by the formality. "I have been asked by the board of trustees to talk to you."

Ron quickly sat up. "About what?"

"Your outburst this morning. They are thinking of suspending you from the hospital."

Ron was tired. He couldn't think. Why was Riggs calling him? Who on the board talked to him? "Look, Carl, I was tired, and she did something stupid. I shouldn't have reacted that way. I'm sorry."

There was a pause on the other end. "Ron. Hopefully, I can smooth it out with the board. But you had better keep it down. Remember, I'm you friend."

"Thanks, Carl." He hung up, relieved.

It took him three weeks to see through the ruse, but it had made him sweat it out during that time. He never heard from the board.

His practice grew steadily but never as well as he thought it should. Once he complained to Steve that Oscar Kansky had a bigger practice, and he was what they called a hacker and duffer. Steve reassured him by asking him if he wanted to be a penicillin and a B12 doc. Kansky gave antibiotics to every kid with a cold that came in with his mother. Ron tried to convince the mothers that the child didn't need them. It took twice as long to explain, and often the mothers left annoyed. They wondered why they had to pay an office visit when they didn't get a prescription.

Many doctors padded their income giving B12 shots to fatigued and anxious patients. The placebo effect was excellent. A big dose of red liquid injected made them feel better. Ron often deprecated the doctors by saying the only thing it did was help pay off their boats. It didn't endear him to some of the medical community.

But all in all, he was developing an upscale family practice where, for the most part, the patients agreed with his philosophy of medicine. The verification came a year later.

"Dr. Campbell? This is John Sailor." The call had come just before lunch. "I'm the new director of the family practice residency at Oceanside." "Hello, Dr. Sailor. I didn't know that Oceanside was starting a family practice residency. They have an internal medicine one."

"Well, in their infinite wisdom, they decided to initiate an FP residency. I've been hired to start it, but I'm a pediatrician and need some boarded FPs to run the clinic."

Family practice residencies were only about five years old. It was an endeavor to elevate primary care from the old GP to a specialty. It was to be a three-year residency followed by an examination leading to board certification. Ron had already become certified following his internship and surgical time in the navy. He'd passed the initial test.

"I think you're the only one on staff who's boarded in family practice and wondered if you'd like to stop by and talk about a teaching position?" Ron was taken aback. It had come out of the blue. The first thing that came to mind was the lease he'd signed, along with the note he was paying off for his equipment.

"You might come on part-time." Sailor cut short his thoughts. "As you know, FP residencies require that the residents spend time in the FP office.

First-year guys work about ten hours a week, second year, fifteen, and third year, almost half time. We're just starting. Since I'm not an office doc, I'm more of an academician, I need someone to run the FP office. As we are just starting, you could be part-time. Any thoughts? By the way, you'll get an appointment at the medical school as an assistant clinical professor."

Ron didn't hesitate. "I'd like to talk to you about it. When can we get together?" He loved the idea of teaching residents, but he couldn't deny that the thought of having an academic appointment was compelling.

That evening he was bursting to tell Barb about the call, but he held back until after dinner and the kids were in bed.

"Had a call today."

"Oh, and just who might that have been from?" She could decipher his tone and knew that the call was either important, good, or hopefully, both. "A doctor, John Sailor." He bled the information out, waiting for her question.

"Ron, stop the BS. What do you want to say? I don't know a John Sailor." Her tone was mocking.

"He happens to be the director of the new FP residency at Oceanside.

He is offering me a part-time position as director of the FP clinic."

Her answer wasn't as enthusiastic as he expected. "You think you can do both? The practice is getting bigger, and you're not home that much now anyway."

He mulled the question over and, formulating his answer, carefully replied, "Yeah, I think so. Initially, it will only be two afternoons a week. It'll give me a chance to get a taste of academic medicine. I may like it. But I have a meeting next Wednesday, and I'll find out more."

"I sure hope that it has a salary. Often these guys think you'll work for nothing."

"I'm certain that they are going to pay," he replied but realized that he hadn't thought to ask. "But what's going on here?" He wondered about her day. "Not much. Got the kids off to school and spent most of the day in the kitchen. My legs are killing me after being on them all day."

"You wear your support stockings like I asked?" After four children, she had developed a significant set of varicose veins. They were worse after standing for long periods of time.

"I put them on after lunch."

"C'mon. They won't work like that. You need to put them on before you get out of bed."

"Ron, I know, but they're so heavy. And it was hot. I don't know what to do."

"Why don't you see Steve? Maybe he'll strip your veins. But that might not be the answer. Check with him. I'll let him know if you'll call."

"I didn't think you liked me having surgery."

"I don't like the idea of having you put to sleep, but vein surgery can be done with a spinal. That's safer."

"Okay, I'll call his office and make an appointment."

CHAPTER SEVEN

On Wednesday morning, he called to confirm his appointment and get directions. He knew his way around the hospital, but the family practice clinic was in an adjacent building. He thanked the receptionist and confirmed that he'd be there at two.

Luckily, he arrived early as parking was almost nonexistent. He had to walk a couple of blocks. He found the office and was not impressed. It was small and somewhat dingy. The secretary was middle-aged and a bit gruff. He introduced himself and said he was there to see Dr. Sailor. She made a call, hung up the phone, and said, "Down the hall. Last door on the right." It was rather perfunctory.

He had worn a suit and tie. But when he met Sailor, the man was   in an open-neck shirt and a long white coat. Sailor stood up and quickly introduced himself. "John Sailor. Nice meeting you, Ron." Campbell was pleased with the informality. "Have a seat." He indicated to the chair opposite the desk.

Campbell did a quick assessment. Sailor was about sixty, sixty-five, trim, and about six feet.

"Thanks for coming. To give you some background, I've only been on the job about three weeks and I am still trying to get my bearings. These things take time to ramp up."

"Where were you before?" Ron was looking for background.

"Well, I'm a pediatrician by training but was running a hospital's graduate education department in the city. That got old quickly, and this came up. And my wife and I wanted out of the commute. So they took me on. They had tried to staff it from in-house, but that didn't work out. That's why I need a family doc to run the clinic. That's where you, hopefully, come in." He smiled.

"Why is Oceanside starting a family practice residency? They have a pretty large internal medicine one."

"Good question. The push now nationally is to open up more primary care residencies. There was funding available from the feds. The board was pushing for it, so here we are. The system, as I might have explained, is that the residents develop their own patients. Families, hopefully, that they follow through their three years. They start a couple of days a week in the clinic and, by their third year, are supposed to spend 50 percent of their time seeing patients in the clinic. We are attempting to staff the clinic with doctors from the community as we go along, but that is a bit uncertain as the internal medicine boys don't think much about the GPs."

"Do you have enough in-patient material to spread around with the internal medicine residents? What do you have, four a year?"

"Six, actually. I think it'll be tight. But we can manage."

Ron was already thinking, *Wouldn't this really fit into Fairtown? We don't have any house staff, and these guys would have almost free reign.* "How do you see me fitting in?" He wanted to hear the details.

"I'd need you to be here two afternoons a week. There aren't any patients signed up as yet, but I think that'll change. Have you done any teaching? By the way, you'd also get a title as an assistant clinical professor at the med school."

"I've had a couple of fourth-year students rotate through my office for their family practice rotation."

"How did that work out? How do you handle them in the office?" "Well, I take them into the room with me to see the patient, introduce

them as a fourth-year student, and ask if the patient would mind initially being seen by them. If the answer is yes, and it almost always is yes, I leave them alone for a few minutes. I then come back in and ask the student to tell me the history and the physical findings. I go over the history, generally ask some more questions, and frequently repeat the examination. We then discuss the case in front of the patient and come to a treatment plan. Usually, I ask the patient what they think about the exercise. I'm amazed that most think it's wonderful. They are impressed with how the thought process works. But then again, I have an upscale practice."

"Excellent. I love that. The student gets some feeling of autonomy but gets critical backup. That's what we are going to need here."

"I have a question." "Sure, go ahead."

"Pardon my French, but this office looks like hell. How are you going to attract patients here?"

"Sorry, forgot to tell you. The hospital is building out an office for us across the street. It'll have six treatment rooms, a small lab, a conference room, and office space for you and me. It should be ready in three months, but I'm not banking on it as you know how these things take time."

"First, are six rooms enough? I have four for myself. Second, who's designing it? Do they have any experience in primary care offices?"

"I asked the same question about rooms. But the space allocated is only so big, and we need a conference room." The second question went unanswered.

"It sounds like family practice is a stepchild." Ron was up-front.

"It may be. But we have applications for next year, actually July, from very good candidates."

"What about the two who are first-year residents?"

Sailor wrinkled his nose. "Not so hot. One is marking time so he can get his license and go into practice. He said he wouldn't be here next year. I think the other resident may leave for a psychiatry residency after this year too. You could be right, but more important is whether you'd like to work with us?"

"I don't know for certain. Is it a paying position?"

"Oh, certainly, how would ten thousand a year sound?"

Ron was taken aback. He had only made thirty-two last year, and this would be for two afternoons a week. He didn't want to counter.

"It certainly seems fair. I think the answer is yes, but I need to run by my wife. She was hesitant because of time commitment. But yes, I think I'd like to start. When do you need me?"

"As soon as you can rearrange your schedule. How about the first of the month? That should give you three weeks. Fair enough?"

"Fair enough. I'll call you tomorrow for a final answer." Ron stood up and shook Sailor's hand. "Call you tomorrow."

As he drove back across the county, his head was spinning. How could he free up another afternoon? How would the ten grand come in handy? Having an assistant professorship was very ego boosting.

"Well, how did it go?" Barb was standing in the kitchen.

"Real well, but I told him that I needed to discuss it with you first." He smiled.

"And?" She was waiting for the rest.

"It'll be two afternoons a week, as well as an assistant professorship at the medical school."

"And?" She was obviously asking about the pay. "Ten thousand a year."

"You're kidding?" She was obviously impressed. "That will come in handy. I think we may have to send Ronald to private school. He isn't doing that well at Elm Street. I had a call from his teacher. He loses interest quickly and is falling behind. They want to start him in a special ed program."

"No way! Once they get into those programs, they never get out. It will stigmatize him forever. Hell, he's seven. I couldn't read at seven. Boys start later than girls. I think you're correct about a private school. Will you look into what's available? By the way, weren't you due to see Steve today?" "I saw him this afternoon.

He was impressed by the set of veins I had. He felt certain that I'd do well with a stripping. He asked me when I wanted to schedule it. I told him I'd talk to you." "Did you ask him how long you'd be laid up?" "He said about a week off my feet."

"How are we going to handle that?"

"I already called my mom, and she said that she'd come down and stay over."

"Wonderful. When?" Barbara's mother was a doll. Ron loved her. He was a lucky one.

"I told her that we would work it out." "Time for a drink to celebrate."

CHAPTER EIGHT

The teaching job worked well from the start. Ron was usually off on Wednesday, "doctor's day," so he added Friday afternoon to the schedule. Sailor was correct that the first two residents weren't very good, but Ron tried to teach them when they showed up. The two knew that they weren't going to be there after July and had very cavalier attitudes. He was waiting to see who had "matched" when March showed up. The so-called match was when fourth- year residents listed their preferences for residency and were computerized with the residency directors listing, in order, who were their choices. Ron hadn't had anything to do with that selection as it had been Sailor's first order of business when he took over. It was a period of anxiety for all concerned.

As well as the teaching was going, the opposite was true of Fairtown's medical executive meetings. They seemed to grow more contentious at every monthly meeting. It was difficult to get anything accomplished. The major contention was Steinshaft. He had failed to recruit another gas passer. The hospital staff had grown with three more surgeons and a full-time orthopedist. That was in addition to the ophthalmology group now becoming three.

It seemed that Riggs and Williams weren't in any rush to push the issue. Ron was convinced that they were blocking English's agenda. Ron had noticed the printed surgical schedule now listed more of Steve's cases than Riggs's. It had to be cutting into his income and perhaps, more importantly, his ego.

Additionally, the fighting had seemed to percolate into the community. English's uncle sat on the executive committee of the board of trustees. He told Steve that the board was hearing things in town. Ron also noticed it when a few patients who needed hospitalization refused to go to Fairtown.

He then lost them to another doctor. When patients and acquaintances said they heard that Fairtown was a lousy hospital, his only reply was that "a hospital is only brick and mortar. It's who takes care of you that matters." It was only partly true. Care required a team effort. The comments he heard only strengthened his resolve to improve the quality of care.

It was late afternoon, and Ron wasn't surprised when Steve called him. They spoke almost every afternoon. Most of the calls were about a humorous incident that had occurred. This time it was a tragic story punctuated with a macabre ending.

"You have to hear this one," Steve started out. "We had our weekly M and M conference this morning." An M and M conference was really about morbidity and mortality. It was a standard conference in every surgical department. As English was chair of the department, he ran the meeting. "A guy about thirty-three, married with two kids, came into the ER about a week ago. Would you believe he'd stuck two lemons up his ass? He didn't have a primary, so they called the surgeon on call." Whenever a patient came to the ER, he listed his primary care doctor. If he needed a surgeon or consult, they called the doctor for a referral. "So the guy on call was Antonio Ramos." He was one of the new additions to the staff. "So what did he do? He sat on him." Steve was using a term that meant watching and waiting. "He passed one of the lemons later that night, but the other was still there three days later. It perforated his rectum, and he died!"

"You're kidding? Why didn't he go after it?"

"No shit. You're an FP and knew that. He's supposedly a board-certified surgeon. I really let him have it. But the funniest part of it was when I got back to my office. I was telling Mary about the case." Mary was his office manager. "Know what her reply was?" He didn't let Ron ask. "'Boy, that case really went sour.'" Even with the tragedy, they both roared. But the humor masked their combined disgust with the quality of care that was being promoted as the "hometown hospital."

After the laughter stopped, Ron asked, "What did Carl say after you went after Ramos?"

"Would you believe he defended him? He said it was an appropriate way to manage the case."

"Steve, he's trying to line up the foreign guys for the next election when the chair of the surgical department comes up for a vote."

"I know that, but I've got to do what's best for the patients. Besides I still have Crazy George breathing down my neck. He damn near accosts me in every surgical case, saying that nobody wants to come here because there isn't enough work. That's bullshit. I came back here last night to see a kid with possible appendicitis. George was sleeping in the surgical lounge. He never goes home."

"What the hell is with him?"

"I asked Bill to let me see his CV, but he refused." A CV was a doctor's résumé that should contain his entire education and work history without times left out. "There's a rumor that he's a Holocaust survivor."

Ron did a quick mental calculation. Assuming Steinshaft's age, he would have been about seventeen in 1944. "So what?"

"The rumor is that he was a kapo." "What the hell is a kapo?"

"Ron! You said that you read a lot about World War II. A kapo was a Jew who worked with the Germans getting the new arrivals into the gas chambers and then taking the dead bodies out for the crematoriums."

"You're shitting me?"

"I said it was a rumor. I can't tell you where it came from." "How did he wind up here at Fairtown?"

"Not certain. He was put on staff before any of us were on board. Williams knows, but he isn't sayin'. It's the same with that idiot we have in radiology, Amos Conforti. They both have come cheap. Remember, when the hospital started, they had to guarantee salaries before they started billing. I'm willing to bet that Conforti is still on salary. He's too dumb and lazy to set up his own billing system."

"That's why every time we ask Bill about replacing him, he balks and says he doesn't have the money. I wonder what he's getting out of it."

"I've asked my uncle Harold about that, but he's closemouthed. You've got to remember that he got the electrical contract for the hospital."

Ron knew when to stop asking questions.

Three weeks later at the next medical exec meeting, they were presented with a surprise. The hospital had received two new applications for the staff, a husband and wife. He was an ENT, and she was an anesthesiologist. Both had excellent credentials. They were quickly accepted on staff. Steinshaft wasn't happy.

Almost as an afterthought, Barbara scheduled her vein stripping eight weeks later. She specifically asked Steve to have Norma, the new gas passer, to be her anesthetist. Barbara detested George.

CHAPTER NINE

The match came through that month. It was a dream. Their four top candidates all matched. They had all grown up within a fifty-mile radius of Oceanside. That usually meant they would stay within the community setting. It was perfect. The three counties were exploding with new families. Ron looked forward to meeting them. He thought that perhaps one might make a good new associate. His practice was expanding. He knew that he would need an additional doctor soon, or he would have to turn away new patients.

Even though the new clinic was behind schedule, it was finished before the start of the new academic year of July 1. It wasn't perfect, but it was far better than the one he had first seen.

The problems started immediately. The family practice residents were sharper than the internal medicine residents. Fighting for cases began on day 1. Unfortunately, Ron wasn't around for the arguments between Will Vance, the head of medical education, and John Sailor. Vance had the power over Chris Thomas, the chief of medicine. Vance aggressively pushed the internal medicine residents even though they weren't as bright as the FP guys. It became ugly.

Ron finally saw an opening. "John, why don't we have the second-year residents spend maybe half their time at Fairtown. We don't have a house staff. They will have a free hand. The place is full of great pathology, and they will see a lot of patients."

"I'm not against it, but what about the doctors? Do any have any teaching experience? Are there any boarded FP or internists?"

Ron was hesitant. "I'm the only boarded FP, and we have a couple of decent internists."

"Are they boarded?"

Ron replied sheepishly, "One is."

"Are you the head of the family practice department?"

Ron knew that he knew the answer. "No, Ken Poorman is." Poorman was an idiot. The department had elected him because they were worried that Ron might become too strong. More importantly, Poorman thought he was capable of teaching residents.

He played his last card. "I think that if you arranged the amalgamation of the residents and Williams was amenable, then you and Oceanside could name me the head of resident education at Fairtown. I could then hook up the residents to those docs that would like the residents to follow their patients. We could keep an eye on the teaching that way. At least they would be following patients that weren't being shadowed by internal med guys like here at Oceanside."

Sailor was, if not a clinical doctor, at least politically savvy. "See if you can set it up. I'm for it if they will let it happen."

Ron was very happy that he had arranged what could be a great teaching experience for his residents. His naivety was quickly made apparent.

Two days later, he called Bill Williams to arrange a meeting. Williams was very amenable and set the meeting for the next morning after Ron finished his rounds. At the meeting, Ron went through all the positives. The hospital would have house staff coverage for about a quarter of the patients, those that were assigned to the teaching doctors, and Oceanside would pay for them. It seemed like a win-win.

Williams listened quietly to the presentation, then posed a couple of questions. "Who is going to cover all the other patients at night?

"Bill, nobody covers them now. At least we would have some coverage." "If we have a doctor in the house, they have to cover all the patients." "Bill! They can't possible do that! They are second-year guys. Twenty or so is enough."

"Perhaps, but we have another problem. Dr. Poorman is the chairman of family practice, isn't he?"

"Yeah, sure." Ron didn't know where this was going.

"Well, he got wind of this and thinks that, as the head of FP department, he should supervise the residents."

Ron was taken aback. "Bill, I thought John Sailor wrote you that I was to head the teaching program. I'm the clinical director of the program."

Williams smirked. "You are at Oceanside. But here you're an attending, and Poorman is head of the department. Let's see how it works out."

"Bill, I'm not certain what you're saying. Are you agreeing with the program?"

"Ron, starting July 1, we will have two residents rotate through here." "Do I get to assign them to the doctors that are going to do the teaching?"

"Sure."

"And I run the program?"

"Not a problem." Williams roared. It was the first time that Ron realized his entire front teeth was a badly fitted bridge.

Ron had spoken to four doctors who were, at least, board eligible, and they were eager to have the residents cover their patients. It allowed them to stay at home when a patient came in the middle of the night, at least one night out of three.

The first few days after the initiation of the residency program, Ron went around checking with the residents and the attendings. Everyone was happy. The problems started the second week. Ted Slowman, a very sharp second-year resident almost accosted him when he got into the doctors' lounge. "I was up all night seeing Poorman's admissions. I didn't think he was on the list of those docs that I had to cover."

"You don't. What did you say?"

"I told him that he wasn't on the teaching staff." "And?"

"He said that I had to cover him as he was head of the department. So I worked them up and did the orders. He never came in."

The only thing that Ron could say was "I'll talk to him."

That talk occurred the next morning in the doctor's lounge. Ron wanted to do it in person. It wasn't something to be done over the phone. "Ken? Can I talk to you for a moment?"

Poorman shuffled over. He wore his stethoscope around his neck wherever he went.

"Ken." Ron wanted to be tactful, not show his strength. "Ted Slowman, my best resident, was upset that you made him see your two admissions a couple of nights ago. He didn't think that was fair."

Poorman sort of grinned at him. Ron finally recognized that he was a passive-aggressive. He wanted to tweak Ron's chain. "He should have. I'm head of the department."

"Ken, you aren't on the teaching staff. You aren't boarded or even eligible. Why should he see your patients?"

"Because they are house staff!"

"No, they aren't. They are here to learn. House staff are paid to see patients. The residents aren't slaves."

That ended the conversation. Ron turned and left the lounge, slamming the door behind. Poorman had gotten to him.

Ron was so incensed that, without thinking the problem through, he went directly to Bill Williams' office. He asked the secretary if he was busy, and hearing his voice, Williams called him in. Before Williams could ask what the problem was, Ron blurted out the conversation with Poorman. After a few perfunctory questions, Williams gave consideration. "You've got to work that out between yourselves."

There wasn't anything that Ron could say. He turned and walked out of the office. It had taken some time, but he finally recognized that Williams was only covering his ass and didn't care what happened concerning the care in his hospital.

CHAPTER TEN

Ron got a call from the ER. He was the guy "in the barrel." It was four thirty, and he had another hour to go in the office. They told him that a sixty-eight-year-old man, who was a diabetic, had a gangrenous foot. His diabetes was out of control. He didn't have a local doctor. *Damn, I've got to go back. I was hoping to watch the football game tonight.* "Is he stable?" he asked the ER nurse. She assured him that he was, and he gave her preliminary orders. "I'll be back around seven, after dinner."

He went home and had a quick dinner with Barbara and the kids. He had to forego his martini. Having dinner was part of the limited time he had to talk to his children and find out about their day.

At seven thirty, he arrived in the ER to find that they had already sent his patient to the floor. He wandered up to Two West and glanced briefly at the chart, noting that at least the patient, Harry Roseman, had Medicare. *At least I won't be working for nothing.* Often patients admitted through the ER to the man on call didn't have insurance. Getting any money from them was almost impossible, as Ron had found out, even when they drove nice cars and had decent houses. He found Mr. Roseman, an obese man, in room 215 near the window. He had an IV running in his left arm. "Good evening, Mr. Roseman, I'm Dr. Campbell. You have been assigned to me." Ron handed him a business card. Roseman read it carefully.

"You're a GP, right?" He didn't wait for a reply. "I was certain that I would get an internist."

Great, just what I need at this time, a smart-ass. "Yes, sir, just a GP. But I'll see what I can do to help you. First, I need some information."

"I already gave them my insurance downstairs."

"Sir, I need medical information." Ron tried to keep his attitude professional. It was getting harder. "You're how old, and when did you first get diabetes?"

Roseman replied, and Ron went through a full medical history, writing it down in the chart. A proper medical history alone could give you a diagnosis almost 70 percent of the time.

"Now, sir, I'd like to take a good look at you if you don't mind." "They did that in the emergency room."

"I'm certain they did, but I need to do a physical too. We can all miss things."

Ron got around to the heart and, rolling the patient on his side, heard a quiet heart murmur. "Did your doctor tell you about a heart murmur?"

"Never, I had a great doctor in the city, and he never mentioned it.

Are you sure?"

Ron, in an attempt to be clinical, realized that the patient was frightened, but his attitude spoke volumes. "When was the last time you saw him?"

"Oh, probably a year or two ago. I'm very busy, so he just reorders my medicines."

"Oh" was all Ron could say. He pulled down the bedcovers to see a very ugly-looking left foot and toes. It was nearly black past the base of the toes, swollen, and two areas were draining. It was gangrene. "How long has this foot looked like this?"

"I dunno. Probably a week or two. I was out of town and didn't pay much attention to it. I only came to the hospital today because my wife saw it when I changed into slippers."

Ron carefully checked pulses in both feet, behind the knees, and in the groin. The only one he found was a faint pulse in the right inguinal area. "You said you didn't smoke, is that correct?" Smoking and diabetes were deadly for vascular disease.

"Well, I don't know."

It was like pulling teeth. "When did you stop?" "About six months ago."

"And how much did you smoke?" He was exasperated.

"About a pack a day for, maybe, fifty years. I started when I was in the army."

Ron pulled the covers back up and sat down in the chair beside the bed. He chose his words carefully. "Mr. Roseman," he started.

"Hey, call me Ted. Only my enemies call me mister." He made a forced laugh.

Ron started again, "Ted, you have a very bad foot. It's called wet gangrene. Most likely it got infected, and that, coupled with very poor circulation from your diabetes and smoking, is going to make it difficult to treat. It's the underlying cause why your diabetes went out of control. The first thing we need to do is get your blood sugar down and see about trying some antibiotics. I'm not certain that will do it."

"What the hell do you mean 'not certain that will do it?'" He was angry. Ron saw that reality was beginning to set in.

"Ted, I'm going to call in a surgeon to look at your foot. After we get some labs back and he evaluates it, then we'll be better prepared to discuss options, okay?"

"Yeah, okay. Who is this surgeon?"

"I'd like to have Dr. English see you tomorrow morning. I'll call him and give him your background."

"Okay, Doc, anything you say. Is this guy any good?"

Ron hated *doc* since the navy. Doc was the corpsman. He was either Dr. Campbell or Commander Campbell. Ron had made lieutenant commander a year before he got out, but navy courtesy was that you called a lieutenant commander, commander. "The best recommendation is that I let him operate on my family."

He told Ted that he would see him in the morning and went to the nurses' station to write up the case and put in more orders. Finally, he called Steve at home and gave him the story. "It certainly looks like he'll need an amputation because of the extent and the circulation, but I leave that up to your profound judgment."

"Go to hell. Go home and screw your wife. You need to blow off some steam. I'll call you after I see him. Anyway, thanks for the case." Steve always thanked him.

Ron went home and took his advice. He felt better.

When Ron was back on Two West that morning, he ran into English. "Did you see Roseman yet?"

"No, I was just going in. Why don't you come with me and introduce me?"

Roseman was eating, sort of, his breakfast. "Boy, is this stuff crap."

Ron smiled. He agreed with Roseman's assessment of the hospital's food. "Ted, this is Dr. English. He wants to see what your foot looks like." Steve introduced himself and shook the patient's hand.

"Mind if I take a look?"

"Be my guest. It don't look so good to me."

Ron had ordered a foot frame so that the covers were off the foot. Steve removed a loose dressing and examined the foot. He then checked the pulses as had Ron. He stood up and looked at the patient. Ron knew what was coming.

"Mr. Roseman, I don't mean to be blunt, but I don't think I can save your foot. There's too much dead tissue, and your circulation won't support it."

"You mean you're going to chop off part of my foot?"

Now came the hard part. "No, sir, in order for it to heal properly, I'll need to go higher, probably about your calf area. That way I can save your knee and get good healing. By saving the knee, a good prosthesis will get you walking again."

"You're shitting me, Doc. Heh, Campbell, I want another opinion." He dismissed English with a wave of his hand. Steve shrugged his shoulders and left the room. Ron waited for the next statement. "Campbell, I don't like that guy. No bedside manner. I'm certain there are better surgeons in this place than that guy. I'm going to call around, and I'll let the nurses know what I decide." Ron knew he was dismissed.

Just after lunch, Patti, his medical assistant, told him that the hospital had called and said that a Mr. Roseman had asked to be transferred to Dr. DeMario, another GP, and that he was off the case. *Oh well. Didn't want to take care of the SOB anyway,* he rationalized.

Two days later, Ron snuck a peek at Roseman's chart. DeMario had asked Carl Riggs to see the patient. Riggs had ordered an angiogram of the left leg. Ron went to the report that stated that patency of the vessels was limited and there was very little, if any, drainage in the foot. It didn't bode well for Roseman's foot. He told Steve about the report that afternoon when they chatted.

"That so? I just got the surgical schedule for tomorrow. Carl is going to attempt a vascular bypass on the guy. Between his inabilities to do vascular work and general surgery, he's going to screw that guy up. Oh well, I told him what had to be done. Wonder what Carl Boy promised him?"

Ron wondered the same thing.

Ron didn't have long to wait for his answer. Two days later, he was visiting a patient who had been transferred into Roseman's room. After seeing his patient, his curiosity got the best of him. "Hello, Ted. How are you doing?"

"Not bad. Just had a vascular bypass by Dr. Riggs, a really smart guy.

Why didn't your friend French or whatever his name was suggest it?" "Perhaps he didn't think it would work." It was the best he could say. "Riggs says that with the bypass, the foot might heal, but the worst would be some amputation of the toes. I made the right choice. See ya, Doc." After two weeks, the bypass hadn't worked. Roseman was still in room 215. Ron

---

didn't bother to talk to him. The following day, Roseman's name showed up on the surgical schedule. He was to have a partial foot amputation. Ron, swallowing his pride, hoped it would work. The following morning, Roseman was in the ICU, diabetes out of control.

"How does that guy's foot look, Ann?" He nodded to Roseman. "He was my patient initially. But when English told him he was going to have BK, he balked and asked for new doctors." A *BK* was short for "below-knee amputation."

"I dressed it this morning. The suture line looks tight, some swelling, and the foot is cold. Not good."

"Keep me posted. I'm worried about him." *Not really. Just nosy and want to see what happens.*

A week later, Roseman was on the surgical schedule again. This time it was for a leg amputation. Ron wasn't certain whether that meant above or below knee. What was interesting about a hundred-and-twenty-bed hospital was that information, both medical and social, was easily obtained. Once again Roseman found his way into the ICU, and Ron realized that he had an above-knee amputation. But more importantly, it seemed that his kidney function was diminished. *Probably secondary to his diabetes, as well as all the surgery,* he thought.

Three days later when Ron visited the ICU, Roseman's bed was empty. "Did the guy in bed 2 go back to the floor?" Ron asked the charge nurse. He didn't want to seem too interested.

"No, Dr. Riggs sent him to Oceanside last night. He said he needed dialysis."

"Were his renal studies worse?"

"Not really, but he was running a temp of 102, and his blood pressure was down. So he sent him at about eight last night."

Ron checked on his patient, wrote some orders, and then figured he had enough time for a cup of coffee. Taking the elevator to the first floor, he found Steve and Bob Garth, the head of OB, there, just about to leave. After some perfunctory hellos, Ron asked Steve to stay a minute. Bob excused himself, saying he had a mother in labor. Ron got a coffee and a donut and sat down at the table. "Remember that patient, Roseman, I had you see? He was shipped out to Oceanside last night. The nurses said Riggs told them it was because of renal failure, but it sounds like he had sepsis."

Ron's tone was of concern and annoyance.

"Yeah, I followed the case on the surgical schedule. I didn't know what happened last night. But that isn't the first time that Riggs has done that. This is at least the third case that I have heard of. You understand why he does that?" "Probably because he doesn't know how to take care of critical cases?" "Well, that may be part of it, but the real reason is that the cases don't show up at mortality conference where his ineptitude would come out.

Simple, huh?"

"Does anyone—you, for instance, as chief of the department—keep statistics about surgical outcomes?"

"Believe it or not, I tried to get the department to set up a simple surgical outcome protocol, but it was voted down almost unanimously.   It went nowhere. Look at it this way. If a baseball manager wants to change his left fielder halfway through the season, he can get the potential replacement's statistics that tell him how well he hits lefties, and how well he plays on real grass and at night. Hell, if a patient wants to know a surgeon's record on, say, colon resections, there isn't a scrap of evidence to give him or her that information. They rely on friends, nurses, and occasionally, their family doc. You've had some surgical training, you understand. But look at the rest of your department. Need I say more? He not only screws up the patient doing surgery he isn't capable of but gets to bill for three separate procedures when he should only be doing one."

"The great American health-care system." Ron shook his head. "Steve, all I know about community medicine is what is going on here. After teaching hospitals and the navy, I'm a babe in arms. Is this all there is?"

"Don't get too discouraged. This place is too new, and maybe Bill is right, not enough grayheads. Not politically but medically. The older guys on the staff are here by default. They were here when the hospital was built. Sooner or later, we'll get some well-trained specialists, but for now, we have to hold the fort."

Three weeks later, in the weekly meeting, Patti told him that Roseman's bill to Medicare had gone toward his deductable. Roseman owed him a bill for the first days in the hospital. Patti informed him that she had billed him but had received an angry call from his wife. She had screamed at Patti, saying that Ron had screwed up her husband, who was slowly dying in Oceanside, and that she wouldn't be paying. If they put her in collection, she would sue for malpractice.

"Don't send her another bill. I'll eat the hundred dollars. I'm sorry about her husband." *But you aren't getting paid.* When a patient came to the office, they paid the bill. It was sort of a contract. But when the patient came through the ER, they sort of expected that the hospital would take care of it.

After dinner that night, he related the rest of the Roseman story to Barbara. She knew up to his departure from Fairtown. He told her about the bill. "I'm thinking of talking to Riggs to see what he has to say."

"Are you crazy? He'll turn it around on you. Don't be surprised if he pushes her to start a suit."

"What? I didn't do anything wrong."

"Who cares? You need a lawsuit like a hole in the head. Put you on the stand, and you'll lose your cool. Stay out of it. Remember, everything that goes around comes around."

CHAPTER ELEVEN

"Ron, you remember that I'm due to have my veins stripped next week? Nana is coming down to help you with the kids. Did Steve speak to Norma about the surgery?" She was referring to Norma Kimball doing the anesthesiology.

"Duh! I forgot, but Thursday is the executive committee meeting. If I don't talk to him before that, I'll make certain to mention it to him."

He didn't have to wait that long. Steve called him Tuesday afternoon about the agenda for the meeting. Before he could start, Ron brought up the subject of Barbara's surgery.

"Steve, did you remember to tell Norma K. that Barbara wants her to do her veins?"

"Yes, I did. I scheduled her for Monday as we discussed. But I have something interesting to tell you. I was scrubbing up this morning for   a gall, and at the sink was Fat Teddy." Fat Teddy was the head of the ophthalmology group. He was Fat Teddy because he was fat and was Ted Cohen. "For something to say, I innocently asked him how the eye instruments were purchased. They use a lot of special stuff. He said that their group owned all the instruments. They had bought them when the hospital opened. So I asked him what would happen if a new, young eye guy came and didn't join their group. He looked at me and laughed. 'Well, he'd have to buy his own.' I was pissed. That's like Riggs owning the surgical instruments. He wants to keep it a closed shop." Steve paused.

"That doesn't sound right to me. But what alternatives do we have?" "I thought about it all day, and here's what I came up with. We give Cohen three alternatives. One, he donates the equipment to the hospital and takes a tax deduction. Two, the hospital buys the equipment at fair market value. Or three, he refuses the first two. So the hospital buys their own, and he can take his instruments to his office."

"Steve, he would be an idiot to refuse one of the two. Ted isn't an idiot, and I think the alternatives are very fair. Have you run this by Bill?"

"No, I haven't had time, but since you ask, I don't think I will. Ted sends a lot of business into the hospital, and I don't think Bill wants to piss him off. I have a feeling that bringing it up fresh at the meeting where it will be heard by all is the best way."

"But Ted doesn't come to the meetings."

"Right, but Thursday morning, I'll have Mary call his office and tell him that I have asked for his input on his department. He'll be too curious not to be there."

Thursday at seven thirty, the executive staff met in the hospital boardroom. The table was full, and a few were sitting in chairs around the walls. Ron was early and got a seat at the table. He needed a place for his coffee and something to write on. The agenda was printed, and under New Business was an item that only said *ophthalmology*. Ron wasn't certain that Steve had discussed it with anyone else. He glanced up in time to see Ted Cohen looking over a copy of the agenda with a quizzical look. He took a seat along the wall but not before Ron saw him quietly talking to Carl Riggs. Riggs just shrugged his shoulders.

After calling the meeting to order and having the reading of the minutes of the last meeting, which required some corrections, the committee finally got around to New Business. Most of the committee was watching English. "The new item that is listed came about concerning a conversation that I had this week with Ted Cohen." He made it sound formal. "Let me attempt to paraphrase it if I might. Ted, correct me if I'm wrong." Not a few stared at Cohen.

"Ted informed me Tuesday that his group has purchased and owns all the eye equipment in the hospital. That is correct isn't it, Ted?" Cohen just nodded. Steve went on, "I then asked what would happen if we had another eye guy applying to the staff and didn't want to join his group. His comment was 'he would need to buy his own equipment.' That is what you said, isn't it, Ted?"

"Steve, we paid good money for that equipment. We're not letting people we don't know use it." It came out in a manner of defiance.

English and the others took that to mean what he had said was on the mark. "Even if I agreed that was okay, can you all realize what a pain that would be for the surgical personnel? They'd have to keep a second complete set of instruments and equipment, microscopes and all else. Then what would happen if a third or fourth person came, all independent? It would be a nightmare. What do you say, Bill?" Steve put it directly to Williams. "Well, perhaps, but we haven't got any new staff ophthalmologists. So it seems moot."

"Bill, it's not moot. Anyone who applies will want to know about equipment. If he finds out that the Cohen group owns it and won't allow its use, then he leaves. It makes Fairtown a closed shop."

"What do you recommend?" Williams had his trademark smirk.

Steve then outlined his three-point suggestion. "I think those are very fair alternatives, any questions?"

Mario Hernandez, chief of pediatrics, asked, "Bill, can the hospital afford it?"

The answer was as usual, noncommittal. "I suppose we could find the money."

Riggs raised his hand, and Steve called on him. "Carl, you want to say something?"

"Steven." It came out almost as a drawl. "I don't think it was fair to blindside Ted like that. You could have discussed it in private."

Ron recognized that Riggs was always trying to get the edge over the other surgeon.

"Carl, you might be correct, but this way everyone knows what the problem is and can be part of the solution." He turned back to Ted Cohen. "Ted, your comments?"

Ted stood up. His shirt was half out, and his nickname became evident. "Steve, I really think Carl was right. We could have done this in private. But I want to talk it over with Bill."

"Before we drop the matter, I want to get the committee's consensus. I'd like to propose a motion that we replace, purchase, or have a donation of the ophthalmological equipment in the OR. Anyone second the motion?"

Ron raised his hand. "I second the motion."

"All in favor?" Ten hands were raised. "Against?" Three hands— Carl's, Mario Hernandez's, and George Steinshaft's. "Then the motion is carried. Ted, why don't you get together with Bill and work out what is best for you and your group. Bill, will you report back to the committee next month what has been decided?"

The only acknowledgement he got was a nod from Bill Williams.

As they left the meeting, Steve and Ron walked out to the parking lot together. "I thought that went better than it could," Ron said.

"Yeah, but let's see what really happens. The three votes against didn't surprise me, but I wonder what they are cooking up."

CHAPTER TWELVE

On Sunday Barbara was admitted to Fairtown for pre-op testing. Her surgery was scheduled for seven thirty on Monday. On Sunday afternoon, Nana had arrived to the great joy of the grandchildren. Ron went in early to the hospital to see Barb before she went to the OR. He had cleared his schedule for the morning. With a spinal anesthesia, she should be out of the OR and into recovery in less than two hours.

He made rounds and then sat in the surgical lounge, waiting for Steve to come out from surgery. At nine thirty, Ron was getting worried. Finally, Steve came in and said, "Everything is fine. She did real well, and I got out the veins without too much trouble. She's going to be a little groggy as she is just waking up."

"Waking up! Norma was going to give her a spinal. What happened?" "Ron, don't get crazy, but Norma wasn't on the schedule. George changed it Friday. He gave her the spinal, but it didn't take. So he had to

put her to sleep. She's okay. She's in recovery."

Ron was out of the lounge by the time Steve had finished his statement. He rushed into recovery, and Sandy Ivey was taking Barbara's vitals. She smiled at him. "She's doing fine, Dr. Campbell. Want some water, Barb?"

Barbara made a loopy grin. "Please?"

"How are you feeling?" Ron's voice had more than a trace of anxiety. "Better now. When Steinshaft came in, I was very angry and almost screamed 'Where is Dr. Kimball?' He said she was off, and Steve said he didn't want to postpone the surgery." "Why didn't he do a spinal?"

"He tried, but when Steve did the first incision, I yelled. I could feel everything. I told that to Steve. He then tested both of my legs, and I could feel all the touches. He then told Steinshaft to put me to sleep."

Ron glanced at Sandy and grimaced. *The sonnavabitch did it on purpose. He wanted to get even with me. Wait until I get my hands on him. Taking it out on my wife.* "Well, it sometimes happens. You're doing fine now. You have a great nurse. Get some sleep. You'll be tired." He wanted to reassure her. He gave her a kiss on the forehead and went back in the surgical lounge. Steve was washing up.

"How's she doing?"

"Fine, but I really think that bastard did this on purpose. I'm going to fry his ass."

"Ron, slow down. It happens, probably one in twenty. They don't take because they miss the mark. Leave it."

"Steve, I don't believe too much in coincidences, but between rescheduling Norma and now this, I'm pretty certain it wasn't happenstance." "So what are you going to do? Kill him?" Steve roared. Ron didn't think it was funny, but he was right. There wasn't much he could do. But he would watch Steinshaft. If he was capable of hurting a patient for revenge, what else was he capable of doing?

Barbara came home in two days and recovered quickly. Her legs felt great, and she was back playing tennis a couple of weeks later. The weeks flew by, and at the next executive meeting, Bill reported that he had purchased the equipment from the eye group. The hospital was full almost daily. The residents seemed to like the environment, and most of the doctors were happy.

At five that afternoon, Ron got his regular update call from Steve, but this time it was different. "Hope you're sitting down for this one. I got a call from Bill this afternoon. He read me a letter from the state medical board. They have a complaint that you and I are fee splitting. Wait! Don't explode. They have to follow up on every complaint. I told him that I would call you and keep you from exploding."

"Who sent it?" The question came out with venom. Fee splitting, meaning the surgeon was paying for referrals, was highly unethical and could be a criminal. It could mean the loss of a license.

"Not yet certain. He didn't say. I'm not certain that he knows. Some are sent anonymously. I'm going over there to talk to him now."

"I'll come with you."

"No, let me see what it's all about. I'll keep you posted." "I think I should call a lawyer. I need to protect myself."

"Keep your shirt on. Nothing is happening. It's just a letter of inquiry. Besides, we don't have anything to worry about. We've never done anything wrong, and even if we had, how would someone prove it? Subpoena our bank accounts? Shit, I don't make enough from your cases to keep you in the lifestyle that you enjoy. I'll let you know more later."

Ron gave a little laugh. He hung up and was seething. *Who the hell did that?* He made a quick mental list but left out one name. That was the one Steve told him that evening.

"I had a long talk with Bill. He talked to Dom Samsom, the attorney for the hospital. I think you know him. He will question the letter writer and then maybe talk to you and me. If there is nothing there, and there isn't, he'll respond."

"Who the hell wrote the letter?"

"Would you believe Fat Teddy? He must have been really pissed because we took away his monopoly. Dom said they could probably wrap this up in a few days. Fortunately, our reputations, other than being drunks, are excellent. Sit tight. Don't get an attorney. That will only stir the pot. If anything comes up, you have time."

Ron was somewhat relieved when he hung up, but he was very angry. Cohen did it for spite. *He probably thought that it would scare us but didn't have the brains to think it through with all the ramifications.* Ron went into the den and, lowering the TV volume, told Barbara the story.

"What are you going to do?"

"Nothing yet. I'm going to wait a few days and keep a low profile. I'll see what Samsom does. I'm beat. I'm going to bed."

CHAPTER THIRTEEN

"Ron, did you see this?" Barbara was reading the *New York Times.*

"I just read the front page. What are you referring to?"

"Here, read this. I seem to remember the name." She folded over the page and handed it to him over the breakfast table. "It's on the left side."

Ron saw the article immediately. The headline was "Mother of Doctor's Wife Accuses Him of Murder." He quickly read down the column and shook his head. Barbara was correct. He knew the name only too well.

The article told the story of how a young doctor, William Stonebreaker, had taken his pregnant wife out in a small boat off Miami and said that they had encountered a storm and the engine had stopped running. He had convinced her to try to swim to shore. He related how the two got out of the boat and tried to swim. He got to the beach, but she didn't and was never found. The article went on to say that the wife's family was very well- to-do and that she had a large trust fund that the doctor was attempting to wrest away from the family. The case was in court.

What struck Ron and Barbara was that they sort of knew the doctor. He was the son of a salesman that Ron's father had hired. Ron had met Stonebreaker a couple of times years ago. Stonebreaker's father had told Ron how smart his son was. That seemed to be proven correct when he was accepted at Penn. But more recently, about a year ago, a new patient had come to his office. And after he had taken care of her problem, she had told him that she was the daughter of the salesman that his father hired, the sister of the doctor. She wanted to know if one of the orthopedists in town was looking for a new associate. Her brother had a year to go in his residency and was looking for a place to have a practice.

Ron told her that he would check around but said that she should have her brother call Jack Mazzola, who had a big ortho practice in town. After that, it slipped his mind. Now he was curious to know what had happened. As soon as Ron got to the hospital that morning after the article was printed, he looked to see if Mazzola was in the hospital. His name was on the board. Ron found him at the nursing station on Two West.

"Jack, did you see this?" Ron had torn the article out of the paper. He handed it to the big doctor.

"Yeah, I knew this was going on. Why?" He had a quizzical look on his face.

"Well, I sort of know him. In fact, his sister is a patient. She asked me about six, eight months ago whether anyone might be looking for an associate. I suggested you. Did he ever call you?"

"So that's how he got my name. Yeah, he came in, and I talked to him. Sort of thought he was a smart-ass, knew more than anybody. I told him I'd think about it and get back. Never did. Thank God I didn't. You know who his father is?"

Ron just shook his head.

"He's in the coffee-vending business in Newark, same place that I grew up. You know what that means?"

Ron wasn't totally naive, but he wanted Jack to say it. "Not really," he lied.

"You aren't in that business up there unless you are connected. That boy stepped into a pile of shit." Jack always liked to allude that he had connections.

"So what happens?"

"So friends of mine told me that he already had had two accidents. One, a garbage truck hits his car. And then two weeks later, a concrete mixer banged into him." He started to laugh.

"From what I hear, he's taking a position down South, maybe Georgia. Could you image if I had told people that I was hiring him and this came out?"

Ron and Jack shared a nervous laugh. But it wasn't funny. A woman and her baby were dead. A three-year-old son was left without a mother. And even if it wasn't murder, it certainly qualified as gross stupidity on the part of the husband. A physician should be able to make intelligent judgments. It upset Ron deeply.

One week later, Steve called Ron and asked him to meet him for a drink at the Inn that afternoon. Ron agreed. But when he asked why,

Steve said he had some news and that it was good but that he wanted to go over it in person.

Ron drove around the corner from his office to the Inn. It was an old colonial structure that served decent, not great, food and had a quiet bar. Steve was already there and had a scotch in front of him. Ron sat down and ordered the same.

"Let's take a booth," Steve said after the bartender had put the drink down. They picked up the peanuts and found a booth away from the two other couples. Ron was getting antsy.

"Well, come on. What is going on?"

"It's all taken care of. Samsom apparently spoke to the fat guy." Steve wasn't using names. "He admitted he didn't have any proof. And I guess maybe the lawyer scared him, and the fat guy said he would write a retraction. So *poof*, it's over. Happy now?"

"What's going to happen to the fat man?"

"Probably nothing. But we might dig up a little something for him." The grin on Steve's face was priceless. "But let's let things ride for a while. *Salud*!" He clinked his glass with Ron's.

Ron was visibly relieved. The charge was behind him, and he didn't need to come up with a couple of thousand dollars that he didn't have for an attorney. But he was still incensed. He had been accused of something that had no basis, in fact, and had gone through a week of hell, upsetting both himself and his wife. And that asshole was walking away. It wasn't fair.

"I'm going home for dinner," Ron said, draining his drink. "You invited, you pay. Besides we're fee splitting." Steve nodded and laughed.

Ron went home, and contrary to his mood, Barbara was upbeat. Before he could tell her about the discussion he just had, she said, "Ron, remember the Doctors Donation Ball that we are going to next month?"

Ron blinked. He had forgotten that the Wives Club had organized the annual dinner dance at the local country club. It was a formal affair and had a silent auction, as well as a dance band. He and Barbara loved to dance.

"Well, I found a gown at Evelyn's today. It fit perfectly, and I brought it home. Want to see it?"

Ron knew he had to acquiesce. She was too enthusiastic. He also knew not to ask what it cost. Barbara was chairwoman of the decoration committee. "Love to. I'll cook the steak, while you show me."

Barbara ducked into the den and came out with a dress on a hanger covered with cellophane. She carefully removed the protective sheath to display a long pink outfit with a low neck. He liked it. "It's very nice. Hope no one else has the same thing."

"Silly. Evelyn knows better than that. Her husband is on the board, and she dresses most of the women. She knows that I'm one of the few that fit into something like this, and she only buys one dress of each style." Barbara was small and very slender. "She's smart enough to know that she'd lose a lot of business if women started showing up in the same outfits. Of course, now I need to find the right shoes."

"Oh, of course." It had a slightly sarcastic tone. But he was very proud of the way she dressed and kept her appearance. Even in casual clothes, she always looked good.

"By the way, just so you don't feel left out, I took your tux to the cleaners and stopped by Roots today and bought you a new formal shirt and cummerbund set. Hope you like them." She repeated the exercise and came back into the kitchen with the shirt-and-tie set. He opened the box and had to admit that the tie and matching cummerbund were nicer than the one he had. The shirt was too.

"They're very nice. I thank you for thinking of me." He bent over and gave her a kiss.

"Heh, I can't have my man going out and not looking the best. I'm proud of that body." She patted him on the stomach. Ron smiled. He tried to stay in shape—running, or really racing, when he had a chance. It was a leftover from his high school and college days when he was a sprinter. He was good, but not great. He knew that since he had run against some of the world's best. He was proud that he even ranked in the same class even if he didn't win. He took the steak out on the wooden board to the already-heated grill in the yard, smiling to himself while remembering some of those days.

While the kids did their homework, Ron finally had time to tell Barb about his conversation with Steve. When he finished, she asked, "You okay now? You've been pretty short the last week. You didn't talk about it, but I knew that it was eating at you."

"Yeah, I'm better but what that slob did—hell, he tried to get my license pulled. That's our livelihood!"

"Well, it's behind you now. Let it go. I know you well enough to realize that you want to get even. Don't. I repeat, don't do anything that will make things worse. You're a doctor. Don't forget that. You are held to a higher standard. Don't embarrass me and our family." She finished by giving him a long stare, her way of driving home a point.

"You're right. But I'm going to Williams tomorrow." "For what?" She seemed concerned.

"I want Cohen disciplined, off the staff actually. He deserves it." "You think that will ever happen? The only ophthalmology guys in town. Do what you want, but don't expect too much. I think you should just let it die."

"Maybe you're right, but I need it for my own satisfaction."

CHAPTER FOURTEEN

The dance was a huge success. The Wives Club made a lot of money for the hospital and was earmarked for the pediatric department to build a new playroom. The food was great, and with the open bar, Ron managed to do a bit too much. Barbara drove home. Ron regretted the dance Sunday morning but managed to watch the Giants get beaten up again Sunday afternoon.

The practice was really beginning to be busy with almost every day filled. He had to increase his staff to three women, making Friday payroll a bit harder. But it was worth it. He had been striving to develop a group of intelligent patients—ones who liked his academic style. It was succeeding. On Father's Day, Barbara, he, and the kids were at Steve's for a small party. Jim Lusk, an internist, and his wife and kids were there too. It was an informal cookout. Ron's pager went off. He went into the kitchen, called the answering service, and found out that he needed to call the ER. *Oh shit! Probably need to go back to see a patient.* He called the ER.

When the ER receptionist came on, she said, "Dr. Campbell, you're on call. We just had a young man come in who fell off his motorcycle, and we think he broke his neck. We need a referral." She was alluding to the fact that since he didn't have a primary doctor, Ron would need to refer him to one of the surgeons who took care of trauma patients. He held his hand over the mouthpiece and called Steve in the den, "They've got a guy that fell off his motorcycle and broke his neck. You want to see him?"

"No, see if Mel Rider will see him." Mel was a neurosurgeon, who rotated between hospitals. Ron took his hand off the mouthpiece and told the receptionist to call Dr. Rider.

The next morning Ron went through the ER and checked to see what happened to the guy who had fallen off his motorcycle. The charge nurse checked the log from Sunday and found the name. "The patient's name was Grotski, and Dr. Rider had him transferred to Oceanside. He was only here about two hours."

Ron thanked her and forgot about the case until two days later when he read the newspaper while having his morning coffee.

The headlines in *Record*, the county paper, screamed in bold letters "Patient Slain in ICU."

Ron quickly went to the body of the article to find that Jim Grotski, his referral to Mel Rider, was shot in the head using a sawed-off shotgun by his own brother, following surgery by Dr. Rider. The brother, Stanley, said he did it as "an act of love." He didn't want his brother to become a cripple. He was in custody in the county jail.

The story went on to tell how the two brothers and Jim's wife lived together on a farm and that they were having a party. Jim decided to ride his motorcycle around the farm and had apparently hit something and fallen off. There wasn't any comment from the police.

When Ron went into the hospital that morning, the case was all that anyone was talking about. But other than the information in the paper, no one had anything more to add. Quickly, the case began to take over the local news. Grotski made bail and went back to the farm. Two weeks later, it was announced that he had hired a well-known criminal defense attorney, Elliot Merman, from a nearby town. Ron and the others wondered where the money had come from, but in the meantime, the publicity had become national news. It was suspected that Merman was pushing the version of a mercy killing to sway any potential jurors. The case would go to court quickly in two months.

Although he was interested in the case—he had been the first called— as well as the sensational murder that occurred in a hospital that he was affiliated with, he had more important things to take charge of, such as his patients and the residents. It didn't come to the forefront until one Tuesday morning, going past the hospital coffee shop, he spotted Mel Rider sitting alone at a table.

Ron ducked into the shop and walked over to Rider's table. "What are you doing here, stranger?" Rider was seldom at Fairtown, especially in the morning. He never did surgery there, and when he visited for consults, it was usually in the evening, long after Ron had left the hospital.

"Hello, Ron. Good to see you too. To answer your question, I came here for coffee after testifying in court this morning." The county courthouse was in the same town as Fairtown.

"Accident case?" Neurosurgeons were either testifying in auto accidents or malpractice. Ron tactfully chose the former.

"No, it was the Gorski case. I was the first witness called." "Really? I forgot that was coming up. What really happened?"

"Well, after I operated on him that Sunday, I told his wife and brother that I didn't know whether he'd be a paraplegic or not. He hadn't severed his spinal cord, and it would be awhile to fully determine his disability. I saw him again Monday and Tuesday mornings, and he was doing okay. He was alert and awake. The next thing I know is I get a call from the ICU about the killing. Boy, that really shook up the nursing staff. Some didn't come back to work for a couple of weeks."

"How do you think the jury took your story?"

"Can't tell, but Merman didn't try a very vigorous cross-examination like I thought he would."

"Do you need to go back again?"

"I'm not certain. The judge dismissed me but said I should be available for further questions."

Ron stood up. "I've got to make rounds but good luck. Not for nothing but better you than me. Have a good day. Why don't we get together for dinner sometime?"

"Good idea. Have Barbara call Mary to set up a date."

Ron left the coffee shop, wondering how, after Rider's story, they could come to a conclusion about a mercy killing.

Four days later he found out. The jury moved to acquit on the grounds of a mercy killing. One juror spoke about how the jury felt. Merman had painted a picture of the two inseparable brothers who loved one another and how Stanley couldn't bear to see his brother suffer. It made great press so much so that within three months, a book hit the market telling the story. But not the whole story—some of which Ron was made aware of a few months later.

It was early Monday evening. Ron had Monday evening hours for some of his working patients. He picked up a chart in the rack before heading into room 3. Bryan Incoma was reading a legal paper. Bryan had been a patient for over three years. He was an assistant prosecutor for the county. "How's it going, Bryan?" Ron shook his hand.

"Just came in because I've been coughing for three weeks and can't seem to shake it. I'm worried that I have pneumonia. We have two small kids at home, and I'm more concerned for them."

Ron asked him a few more questions and then asked him to remove his shirt. He wanted to get a good listen to his chest. He disapproved of doctors listening to hearts and lungs through their shirts. After a few minutes, Ron said, "Put your shirt on. Your chest is clear. Sometimes after a virus, you have a persistent cough for a couple of weeks. I can prescribe a strong cough medicine if you need it to sleep."

"No, thanks. I'm good. I just wanted to make sure."

Ron finished up his notes, looked up, and asked, "What really happened in that Gorski case? I was the referring doctor to Rider."

Incoma snorted. "That was screwed up from the beginning. I was furious. No one from the sheriff 's office or our office ever investigated what went down. I suppose you know that the brothers both lived together with the victim's wife? Who says

Stanley didn't get hit with a two-by-four or a crowbar? You know what happened after the case was decided?"

Ron shook his head in the negative.

"The brother and the ex-wife sold the farm posthaste and together moved out of state. Ask my opinion, I think he did it."

"And there isn't any way that he can be tried again, right?"

"You hit it, Doctor. That's exactly correct." Incoma shook his head in disbelief. "But anyway, thanks for the good news. Now I can go home and tell the old lady. She's been busting me to see you."

"Do you need a note, Prosecutor?" Ron was ribbing him.

"No. I'll show her the bill, smart-ass." He shook Ron's hand and left. Ron suddenly realized that he had never thought of the possibilities behind the killing. Medicine could be complicated at times.

CHAPTER FIFTEEN

Ron and Steve were having lunch in the cafeteria. They were seated at the end of the table, talking quietly. A number of the doctors had asked Williams to specify one table as a Doctors' Only, but he had steadfastly refused. It wasn't question of being "snobs," as Williams had accused them, but of confidentiality. Doctors liked to get informal opinions and discuss medical cases, but with just anyone sitting in close proximity, that couldn't happen.

Ron had just finished telling Steve about his meeting with Williams that morning. Ron did what he had told Barbara he had wanted to do. When he told Williams that Cohen should be off the staff, Williams just laughed. He patronizingly said he'd think about it.

"You don't, in your wildest dreams, think that's going to happen, do you? Eye surgery is big moneymaker for the hospital. It's clean and doesn't require intense nursing care. Williams isn't going to let that slip by because of a little thing like ethics."

Ron was chastised. "I just needed to say something," he said, somewhat contritely.

"Ron, I almost forgot. I hope you don't mind, but I asked Ted to take a look at a case I did three days ago." He was referring to Ted Slowman, a second-year resident. Normally, the family practice residents didn't see or follow surgical cases. Slowman was a really sharp young doctor.

"Oh, why?" Ron was a bit surprised.

"I did a partial gastrectomy for a bleeding ulcer on a woman, a case that Lou Z. sent me. She seemed to do well, but she slipped into a coma yesterday after she was up and sitting in a chair. I went over all her labs, but nothing indicates why she went sour. Thought a fresh brain on the case might help. You know Lou wouldn't have a clue." Lou was an old-fashioned GP, who couldn't handle up-to-date medicine.

"What did Ted think?"

"His first thought was that she had liver failure, but when all the studies came back from the lab, they were all normal. It really seems strange that we can't find anything."

"Who gave her gas?" Ron was questioning who the anesthesiologist was. "Norma. Everything seemed to go fine. I was in and out in just under two hours.

Two hours for a gastrectomy was excellent time. "So what happens now?" "The family, her daughter and son-in-law, said they were calling in a big doctor 'from the city.'" Many of the residents of Fairtown were émigrés from the city and felt that medicine must be better there. They all referred to doctors there as "big men." Ron always felt like asking "How tall?" But he held his tongue. Steve was once asked if he knew the "big man." His reply, he told Ron, was "No, does he know me?"

"What kind of specialist? Neurologist?"

"That would make sense, but I put my foot in my mouth and said it might be liver failure. So they just happened to know a liver specialist and have asked him to see her. Since he doesn't have privileges here, I told the family he could have temporary ones." Steve could do that since he was the chief of staff.

"Did they say when he would be here?"

"Tomorrow afternoon. I asked Ted to present the case. I hope that's okay with you?"

"Not a problem. I think I'll stick around since I don't have office hours tomorrow. Was planning to go home and work in the yard, but this will give me an excuse." He grinned at Steve. He wasn't looking forward to raking leaves.

The following afternoon, Ron got to the ICU before two, the time of the consultant's arrival, and went over the chart. He wanted to get a feel of the case prior to his resident presenting it to the "big doctor from the city." At twenty minutes after two, while the three doctors were in the waiting area, the elevator door opened, and a thirtysomething female came striding down the hall. She wore a tight-fitting skirt, blouse, and high leather boots. Steve glanced at Ron and Ted and quietly whispered, "Looks like something from 42nd Street." He was referring to the oldest profession in the world.

"Dr. Weiland?" There was a question in Steve's voice. They had all assumed the "big doctor" was going to be a man.

"Yes, I'm Dr. Weiland." She never offered her first name.

Steve proceeded to introduce himself, Ron, and Ted Slowman, the resident. "Ted will present the case, if you don't mind?"

They all took seats in the lounge except Ted, who stood, and by memory, over the next ten minutes, presented the case in detail. He then asked if she had any questions.

"What were her liver studies again?"

Ted reeled off the numbers without referring to the chart. They were all well within the normal range. Weiland then asked whether certain other laboratory tests had been done. The tone was "Did you guys in this little hospital know what to order?"

Ted then presented the test results she was asking about, again without referring to the chart. They too were all normal.

Dr. Weiland stood up and brushed down her skirt. "It's time to examine the patient."

Steve opened the door to the lounge, held it, and let the lady go first. As Ron passed, he wrinkled his brow as if to say "We're mere children." He walked the group into the ICU and pointed to the first bed where the poor lady lay in a coma.

Dr. Weiland walked to the side of the bed, took out a stethoscope, and then did a perfunctory examination. Ron wondered how much the family was paying for this farce. "Let's go look at the x-rays," she said.

It reminded Ron of what it was like to be a third-year medical student. The four physicians took the elevator into the basement where radiology was located. Thankfully, Ted had thought they might be looking at films, so he had the x-ray envelope handy. It was almost an inch thick.

"Any particular study you want to see?" Ted asked. "Let's start with the chest films."

Ted did a short inventory and put the films down on the desk. Dr. Weiland's next action prompted surprise. She put the chest film up backward. Steve glanced at the two others, leaned over to the view box, popped the film out, turned it the correct way, and put it up. "We view chest films this way out here in the boonies." It was bitingly sarcastic, but she didn't bat an eye. Slowly she went through a number of films. It was approaching an hour.

Finally, after all the x-rays had been put back into the jacket, Steve finally asked, "Well, Doctor, what do you think? The family is in the patient's lounge. I'm certain they want your opinion."

"Well, I think she's in liver failure."

"With all her liver functions normal?" Ted was incredulous.

"I've seen a case or two. I know it's a long shot, but I think we should give her a Kayexalate enema." Kayexalate was being used to lower liver by-products.

Dr. English had enough. He had hoped to get some real advice about a terrible case. What he had gotten and, the others had lost time on, was a joke. "Doctor, you're going out there to tell that family that you're going to give their dying mother an enema and she'll wake up? Shit, that's what my grandmother would say."

It took all of Ron's self-control not to laugh. He needed to get away from this comedy. "Steve, Ted, I've got to go. I have patients. I'll call you later." He hurried out of x-ray and into the parking lot, where he let himself let out a roar of laughter.

It took him some time to get the grin off his face, but when it did, it became a grimace. Ron was wrapped up in the details of the case and hadn't thought of the big picture. It struck him that the case was similar to that of Nora Cheerman. He didn't want to become too conspiratorial, but who was in the ICU before this woman went into a coma? He needed to know just to satisfy his curiosity.

Steve called him later that afternoon, and they laughed about the consultant. He told Ron that she did tell the family about the enema, and they seemed satisfied. Ted was doing the procedure as they spoke. Ron did not share his new thoughts with Steve. *Better to get some evidence first.* Early the next morning, he got to the ICU just after the nurses had changed shifts. He noticed that the first bed was empty. He sat down next

to Ann Ciardi at the nursing station. "She died?"

"Yes, the girls told me she did. About two this morning." "Anyone ask for a post?" Ron was referring to a postmortem.

"I think Dr. English asked the family yesterday if we could have one if she died. They were pretty vehement in saying no. They were Jewish and didn't want to go through that."

Ron shook his head. "It would have been good to know what happened. Ann, who was working when she went into the coma?" It wasn't exactly tactful, but he didn't care.

She looked at him carefully. "Are you suggesting that one of my staff was responsible?"

Ron hadn't meant that at all but knew the way he asked the question was inappropriate. He hadn't wanted to get so far into the question but needed to answer her. "I wasn't implying that at all. I was . . ." He just trailed off.

"As a matter of fact, I was on, along with two other girls. We had our hands full. There was a really sick patient in 3, and then the patient in the isolation room coded. It was a bit of a madhouse for over an hour."

Ron knew the answer to his next question. "Who ran the code?"

"It was just before three, and the only doctor who came and ran the code was George." The way she was looking at him was a question.

"And did the code survive?"

She just shook her head. "With George?" It was an answer.

"And then you found that the patient in bed 1 had gone into a coma?" "Well, we were all so busy cleaning up and looking at the other patients that it wasn't until after shift change, we were all still here, that one of the girls found her unresponsive. I called Dr. English, and he asked if that resident Ted Slowman was in the house. I paged him, and he called English. English said that Slowman would see the patient." She paused. "Are you suggesting what I think you are?" It was said with a piercing look. Ron waited. He was afraid of what he could say. "Just wondering. Remember Nora Cheerman? It was just a year after we opened? The two cases look too similar."

"Ron." She never called him by his first name in the ICU. "I hear you. I have been having similar thoughts for a time. What could I do? I'm a nurse, and who would believe me? All the bad codes and two that were English's cases. Everyone knows that George hates him but . . ." She ended it.

"Ann, I'm the supposed head of the ICU, but who do I take it to? Steve? He's the chief of staff. Everybody will say it's a conspiracy. The only thing to do is to see if it happens again." It was the best he could do. Driving back to his office, all Ron could think about was "if it happens again." *What happens? Another patient dying under unusual circumstances? Then what do I do?* He began to ruminate about all the codes that hadn't succeeded and then the two patients of English. All signs pointed to Steinshaft—that, coupled with Barbara's "botched" spinal from the bastard.

He didn't think he was a conspiratorial person, but the circumstances certainly pointed to a very dark corner.

CHAPTER SIXTEEN

It was the Thanksgiving weekend. Ron cut his Friday office hours to just the morning and closed on Saturday. He would pay the piper on Monday when he'd be busier than ever. It was also the week that the hospital staff would elect new, or reelect old, chairmen. They would also elect the new medical board, including the chief of staff. Ron figured that Steve would be reelected.

Once again, although Ron was nominated to be chairman of the family practice department, he was defeated by Poorman. He was elected as the at-large member of the board. Steve was reelected as chief of surgery. The following Thursday, the department heads, as well as the at-large members, met in the boardroom. There didn't seem to be more than elections on the agenda. Steve brought the meeting to order. "Since we're into the holiday season and we all want to get home, how about we dispense with minutes and any old business? Any objections?" There was a general consensus as affirmed by grunts and raised hands.

"Let the record show that we approved the minutes by unanimous vote. Now I guess we have to move to the election of the chief of staff. Do I hear a second?"

"Well, I'd like nominations for the position of chief of staff." English looked around the table. Bob Garth raised his hand, and Steve called on him. "I'd like to nominate Steven English to be chief of staff again."

Steve smiled and asked for a second. Ron raised his hand, and Steve nodded at him. "I second the nomination." Everyone in the room had expected that.

"Any other nominations?" He looked over the room. Slowly Riggs raised his hand. "Carl?" Steve asked.

"Yes, Steven." Riggs was his pontifical self again. "I nominate Mario Hernandez." There was quiet in the room. "Seconds?" Steve asked.

"I second." It came out as a wheeze from George Steinshaft.

Ron was suddenly looking around the table. He could swear he saw some smirks. He wondered what it meant. He began to count heads. Of the eighteen voting members, he saw that six were foreign trained. He made an assumption that they had gotten together to vote as a bloc. That meant they only needed four more to vote for Hernandez, who, although from Puerto Rico and a United States citizen, was still foreign. Ron wondered if Riggs had maneuvered the vote.

"Any other nominations?" English's voice betrayed his emotion. Ron was certain he had done the same math. "Since there are no further nominations, I will move to have the nominations closed. Any objections?" A few shook their heads to indicate to proceed. "Nominations closed. Do we vote by a show of hands?"

"No, a secret ballot is correct." Hernandez was going to protect his friends.

"Okay then, a closed ballot. Could someone provide eighteen pieces of paper for the vote, and then we need three people to count the votes. Volunteers, suggestions?"

After some suggestions, three of the board was chosen. The paper ballots, or more reasonably called scraps of paper, were distributed to the voting members. It didn't take long for everyone to write out his nominee and fold the paper to secure the identity. They were passed to a side table where the three vote counters put them in a pile and scrambled them, attempting to keep the voter identities concealed. The tabulation didn't take long. They repeated it to be certain, and Norma Kimball, one of the counters, announced the winner, "Tonight the staff has elected Mario Hernandez as the new chief of staff. Congratulations."

"Could we have the actual count please?" Ron wanted to get an idea of what was going on.

"Does anyone have any objections?" Kimball asked, searching the room. When no one objected, she said, "The vote count was eleven to seven." She breathed a sigh of relief and sat down.

"Well, congratulations, Mario. I will cede the gavel to you for the following year. Best of luck." Steve gave him a nice applause that the table joined in with. "I suspect that ends this meeting. Any objections?"

"Hold on, Steve, we need to elect a secretary." Garth had come alive. This time there wasn't any intrigue. No one really wanted to be secretary. It wasn't a stepping-stone to the chair, as had just been realized.

Norma was unanimously elected. In 1975, women were still thought of as secretaries. The meeting was finally adjourned.

Ron and Steve found themselves, along with Bob Garth, outside the meeting room, reviewing or commiserating about the vote, when they were approached by Bill Williams.

"Well, that was a surprise." Williams grinned at Steve. "But I guess all good things must pass." Everything Williams said came out as sarcasm. "But look at it this way, now I have someone that I can work with." He turned and left the group, who all had their jaws, figuratively, gaping.

"Did I just hear what I think I heard?" Garth said. "What a schmuck." "Nice way to end an evening. I'm going home." Ron stomped out of the hospital.

He told Barbara what had happened, but he cut short any discussion. He needed time to think. He sat in the living room by himself, listening to his extensive sound system and thinking about what had just happened. The thought that George Steinshaft now had Hernandez as his protector almost made Ron sick. It just couldn't end well.

CHAPTER SEVENTEEN

The changing of the guard at the chief of staff position brought an addition to the hospital. Her name was Maria Tern. When Ron first saw her, she was swishing down the hallway in a clinging dress and heels. She looked to be in her late forties but was dressed much younger. The look exuded sex and knew it. She looked over Ron and Steve as she went past as though they were part of a meat market.

"Who the hell is that?" Ron asked.

Steve laughed. "That's Maria Tern. She just started as a secretary or something. She was Hernandez's office manager. When he began as the chief of staff, Bill hired her. It makes one wonder, doesn't it?"

"What's in it for the two of them?"

"I don't really know, but I'll tell you a story that I've never told anyone but my wife. It was just after I moved back to town and opened my office. I got a call from Hernandez, and he asked to get together. I thought, heh, maybe I'll get some referrals. Pediatricians don't find much surgical pathology, but when you're hungry, a case is a case.

"I invited him up to my house for a drink, and we sat around chatting.

Odds and ends, but he made certain to tell me that he had eight kids." "Eight kids? All of them his, or is it a blended family?"

"Not certain. He was careful about not saying much about his prior background, where he went to school, or anything else. Oh, I did find out he had moved here from Florida, but he never said why. Then he talked about how two of his children were soon going to be starting college and how much that was going to cost."

"Uh, oh. I see where this is going."

"Perhaps, but what he did was very clever." Steve paused. "He asked me for a loan. Five thousand to be exact. First, I didn't have five grand. And second, more importantly, I knew that I'd never see that money again. It was a payoff for him and his partner to send cases."

"What happened?"

"I tried to be as tactful as I could. I still wanted their work, but I wasn't going to pay referral fees. That, as you so rightly know, is illegal. I told him that I didn't have any money, just starting the practice and buying a new house. I lied and said that perhaps in the future we might work something out. He left on, what I thought, pretty cordial relations, but it stuck in my craw."

"Did anything come of the conversation?"

"Well, about six weeks later, he called me, saying that he had a six- year-old that he thought had appendicitis and asked if I would see her. So he sent her to the ER where I examined her, confirmed his diagnosis, and called him to tell him that I was taking her to the OR. She did real well. The parents were happy as hell, and she went home in three days. In fact, I saw the father about two, three months ago for hemorrhoids, and he thanked me again."

"So that's it?"

"Not really. About a week later, Hernandez caught me in the cafeteria and brought up the case. He implied that we had a deal. I fudged and said I didn't remember 'a deal.' He walked away in a huff."

"Never saw another case again I bet?"

"You got it. All his surgery, what there is of it, goes to Riggs. As you just said, I wonder what's in it for them."

Ron remembered back to his first encounter with Hernandez, or more appropriately, a case of his. He had just been in practice three or four months when a young couple brought their six-week-old into the office. It was about seven at night, and Ron was just ready to leave. He saw a few tiny tots but wasn't all that comfortable treating sick ones. As one of his pediatric professors had said, "They get better real fast and sick real fast." He took a history and found that the parents were concerned that the baby was crying all the time and wasn't gaining weight. They had been seeing a pediatrician, Hernandez, as Ron found out, and the day before, had started him on Donnatal, an antispasmodic for the bowel. It hadn't done anything to stop the crying.

Ron put the child on the baby scale and, after a discussion with the mother, found that in six weeks, the child had gained less than a pound. The belly was distended, and he was arching his back. He looked very sick. Ron listened to his heart and lungs, felt his abdomen, and found very little to justify the baby's condition.

"How much formula is the baby taking at each meal?" "Oh, he's not on formula. I'm breastfeeding."

Ron's ears perked up. "Are you certain he's getting enough milk?"

She looked a bit sheepish. "I'm not certain. I'm not leaking, and my breasts don't feel full. What should I do?"

The father's eyes were boring in on Ron. He looked terrified.

"Why don't we try something simple? How about going to the store tonight and getting some formula? I don't really care which brand, and see if he'll take two or three ounces. Call me at home tonight after you try that. And by the way, stop the Donnatal."

Ron usually didn't give out his home number, but he was concerned about the child. He had his answer three hours later. The father had called to say the baby took all three ounces and fell asleep. He sounded delighted. Ron told him about a feeding schedule and asked to see the baby in a week. When the week came by, the child had gained a little over a pound and was no longer crying. He felt like a hero and remembered the saying "take an appropriate history." He always wondered about Hernandez after that.

CHAPTER EIGHTEEN

"Heh, you won't believe this." It was Steve calling Ron on what had become an almost regularly scheduled call before they left their offices in the afternoon.

"What won't I believe? After the last few years, nothing would surprise me. But go ahead."

"Remember that broad Maria Tern, the one that was Hernandez's secretary and now works at the hospital?"

"Yeah, and?" He was waiting for Steve to get to the point.

"She's apparently having a thing with both Hernandez as well as Tim Baken. Can you believe that?"

Tim Baken was the head of the board of governors. They, along with Bill Williams, set policy, wrote and approved contracts, and hired and approved the senior management, including the hospital administrator.

Baken was a wealthy man owning a chain of auto parts stores. He was one of the three or four movers and shakers that had been instrumental in founding the hospital. He was well into his fifties and had grown children. He was still married.

"Really? Where did you hear that?" Ron was a bit skeptical.

"It came from a real reliable source, my uncle. He's on the board, and it seems that the story is making the rounds. So it might not have been Hernandez that got her the job but Baken. That would make more sense since I don't think Hernandez has any real clout with Williams.

"To add to the story, Baken's wife found out and told him she was going to leave him if he didn't break it off. The best part is that she owns almost all the stock in the company and threatened to can his ass and put their son in charge." By this time, Steve was laughing through the narrative. "Oh, our little hospital is a regular *Peyton Place*."

"What else is new?" Ron wanted to get home.

"Remember we talked about our friend Fat Teddy and how we owed him one?"

"Sure, and?"

"Well, I was in town today and had to park in the lot behind the stores. So when I went around to the pharmacy, I went by that store that sells used items. And guess what they had in the window? An old typewriter. Not an antique but just used. I went in, and the guy let me try it out. And it worked okay. It was fifteen bucks, so I bought it."

"What for?" Ron was puzzled.

"I thought we could get together and compose a little missive to Cohen's wife. Say about Teddy and his girlfriend."

"He has a girlfriend?" Ron hadn't heard that before. "That fat slob has a girlfriend? Who'd want him?"

"Schmuck! I don't know whether he has a girlfriend but then that witch he's married to doesn't either. I just want to give him a dose of what he put us through. It'll do my heart some good. I thought you might like to also. So I bought a typewriter that can't be traced to either of us. After we use it, we toss it. I thought for fifteen bucks, we couldn't go wrong."

Now he had Ron's attention. "Great idea. Are you in your office tomorrow afternoon? I can stop by, and we can compose something." Ron remembered his pledge to Barbara. But an anonymous letter? It would give him some closure.

"I'll be there all day doing paperwork. Come by when you're finished at the hospital." Steve, like many surgeons, had an office in close proximity to the hospital.

"See you tomorrow. I love the idea." Ron left his office with a smile but knew he couldn't tell a soul.

The following day, Ron left the hospital and walked across the street to Steve's office. As he walked in, Arlene, Steve's secretary, looked up in surprise. "What brings you slumming, stranger?"

"I was in the neighborhood and thought I'd stop by. Steve and I have some hospital business."

"I bet. Some funny business?" She smiled, and Ron wondered if Steve had said anything to her. She was quite good-looking and was very personable. For a fleeting moment, Ron wondered if Steve had anything going with her. "He's in his office. You can go in. He doesn't have any appointments."

"Thanks." But Ron already knew that. He found Steve in his private office, entered, and closed the door. "So where's the notorious typewriter?" He was glancing around the office as he sat down opposite the desk.

"In the trunk of my car. I didn't want to bring it in here while Arlene was in the office."

"The way she greeted me with 'funny business' made me wonder if you had said anything to her."

"Nooo, not a word. But I heard that crack she made to you. She's almost ready to leave, but we can get the wording down."

They spent the next hour composing a letter that was, they felt, generic enough to hide the writer's identity. It followed the format of all those types of letters informing the wife of the dastardly doings of a wayward husband without naming names.

Halfway through the exercise, Arlene knocked on the door and told Steve the phone was turned over to the answering service and that she was leaving for the day. Steve thanked her and said he'd see her the next day. After she had been gone for ten minutes, he left the office by the back door and went to his car. He returned with an old Smith Corona typewriter, a ream of paper, and a small box of envelopes.

"Why the paper and envelopes?"

"So it's not on the stationery I use in the office. Boy, you are dumb." He jumped up and went into an examining room and came back with two pairs of surgical gloves. "Don't need to have our fingerprints on any of this." He handed Ron a pair and indicated that he put them on.

He set the typewriter on the desk, inserted a sheet of paper into the machine, and pecked out the wording they had written down. He made certain to make two spelling mistakes and one *x* over. He pulled the printout and handed it to Ron. "What do you think?"

Ron quickly read over the copy—it was only two paragraphs—and silently nodded his approval. Steve took that as a go ahead, inserted it into an envelope, and stopped short. "Heh, stupid," he said to himself, "I don't know the number of his house. I know the street but not the number." He pulled open his desk drawer and found the medical staff roster. It had home telephone numbers and addresses. He flipped the correct page and found the number.

He finally typed in the address and pulled the envelope out. "Fold the letter, and put it into the envelope, while I get a stamp from Arlene's desk."

Ron did what he was told and sealed it.

When Steve came back, Ron said, "What are you going to do with the typewriter now?"

"I'm going by the post office on the way home. I'll put the letter in the box outside, and there's a Dumpster in the parking lot behind. If no one is around, I'll toss it in there, along with the stationery. One last chance, do we mail it?"

It took Ron a bit to consider. "Damn right. That SOB wanted to have my license revoked. He was happy to take away my livelihood. He deserves it. Mail the thing."

CHAPTER NINETEEN

"Doctor, there's a lawyer on line 1 who wants to talk to you." Patti, his office manager, was calling from the front desk.

"Did he say what it was about?" Ron was spooked since the Fat Teddy episode.

"No, he just said that he had to talk to you."

"Okay, thanks." Ron picked up the phone and pushed line 1. "Dr.

Campbell, can I help you?"

"Dr. Campbell, my name is Vernon Raymond. I understand that you do malpractice evaluations?"

Ron had done two or three malpractice evaluations. In fact, he had done one for a lawyer who had a client that he had won over five million dollars for against the city of New York.

"Yes, I do malpractice evals, but let me tell you my rules before we start. If I find malpractice, I will tell you. If there isn't any malpractice, I will tell you. I'm not going to bend the rules to fit your case. Agreed?"

"Absolutely, it wouldn't be profitable if I disagreed. What do you charge?"

Ron smirked to himself. They always think in dollars. "For a straightforward case, two hundred and fifty dollars. For that, I will provide a written report."

"Fair enough. If I get the reports to you, how long will you take to give me an answer?"

"I can give you a verbal reply in a week if the chart isn't too long. The formal report will take longer as I will need to write it up and have my staff type it."

"Deal, it will be there this week. I'm sort of running out of time as the case is almost two years old."

Ron remembered that cases needed to be filed within two years. "I'll try my best to expedite it, Mr. Raymond." Ron liked these cases. He could see what other doctors were doing, and the money was always welcome.

Two days later, he got an express mail package that contained two office notes from two different family doctors and a larger package from Oceanside hospital. He was familiar with the two FPs. They were okay docs. The copies weren't the best, but he was able to get through them. Apparently, the patient, now the claimant—Ron had to think in legal terms—had gone to see one of the GPs on a Monday. He was diagnosed with a cold and was given penicillin. He didn't get better and, three days later, saw the second GP, who was covering for the patient's primary. He was continuing to cough, and so he was sent for a chest x-ray. The reading on the x-ray showed a pericardial effusion. The pericardium is a tough lining around the heart, and the effusion, or fluid, had infiltrated into that area. Pericardial effusions can be caused by a number of things but most commonly by a virus. A cold.

The covering doctor admitted him to Oceanside. He asked Ron Gillip to see the patient.

Ron Gillip had joined the staff at Oceanside just about a year or   so earlier. John Sailor had been extolling his training to Ron. Ron was skeptical. Why would a cardiac surgeon who had trained with the great Dr. DeBakey in Houston want to come to Oceanside when they didn't have a heart-lung machine and weren't going to get one as the state regulated who got the top-level equipment? They were called certificates of need.

Since then, Ron, although he didn't spend much time at Oceanside, had heard rumors that Gillip was doing a lot of questionable surgery.

Ron read the report from the hospital. On arriving in the ER, the patient was never deemed or recorded to be in significant distress. The history and physical never documented any major problems. That evening Gillip took the patient to the OR and opened his chest and cut open the pericardium. He "windowed" the heart. He never attempted to drain the effusion with a needle and, after the operation, never sent a piece of the pericardium to the laboratory for evaluation.

Ron was certain that this was either malpractice or just plain greed. He could have waited and seen what medication would have done. He sorted through the paperwork and found Raymond's telephone number. He dialed and was connected to the lawyer. "Mr. Raymond, Ron Campbell. I wanted to talk to you about the case you sent me."

"Great, what did you find?"

"I think you have a case of malpractice or, at least, improper treatment. Dr. Gillip should never have operated on your client that night. There were other things he could have undertaken long before splitting his chest."

There was dead silence on the phone. "Did you hear me, Mr. Raymond?" Ron wasn't certain the line hadn't gone dead.

"I heard you. The client thinks that Gillip saved his life. He thinks the GP fucked up."

"You're kidding? The worst thing that I can say about the GP is that he gave your client an antibiotic for a cold. You can't do a chest x-ray on everyone who has a cold without other problems. The second guy just happened to get lucky. Nothing in any of the records, including the hospital notes, indicate that the pericardial effusion was life-threatening. It was just the x-ray but no physical findings or history."

"Fine. Send me your bill." It was terse, and Ron was aware the attorney was annoyed. Then the line went dead.

Ron was bewildered. He'd given the attorney a proper evaluation and had been rebuffed. He picked up the phone and called Steve.

"Yeah, what's up?" It was the type of communication that close associates utilized.

"You've got to hear this." Ron spent the next ten minutes reiterating the case to Steve. He needed to vent.

"And?" There was a pause. "Gillip is an asshole. I never told you this, but about three months ago, I had a patient from one of the guys with thrombophlebitis. We were treating her conservatively, and she was getting better. Her kids came down from the city and wanted to have a 'real' vascular surgeon see her. Hernandez gave Gillip temporary privileges, and he came to see her. I was there. He did a perfunctory examination and then said to me that I should strip her veins."

"What? That's contraindicated in thrombophlebitis. You know that, and you're a GP." Steve always used the epithet GP when he meant it as a compliment. "What did you say?"

"I told him that if he thought she needed her veins stripped, then he could have her transferred to Oceanside and do the surgery there."

"What happened?'

"I don't know what he said to the family, but she's still here and getting better."

And life went on.

Three weeks later, Ron, along with John Sailor, was working with the residents in the conference room. Ted Fast had just seen a man who, after working in the garden, had developed a significant rash secondary to poison ivy. Ron listened as Fast described his treatment plan. Ron nodded his approval. Then Fast asked about anti-allergy shots for poison ivy.

"They aren't indicated and don't work," Ron replied. "Are you certain?" Sailor responded.

"Yeah. They are skin-modified allergens. They don't respond to hyposensitization."

"Let's check with one of the allergists," Sailor insisted. "Know anyone we can call?"

"My youngest son sees an allergist who's on staff here. I'll give him a call."

Ron dug into his briefcase, got his phone book, and looked up the number. He picked up the telephone on the table, dialed the number, and when connected, told the secretary his name and asked to speak to Sam Watson. She put him through.

"Dr. Watson, Ron Campbell."

"Hello, Ron, what can I do for you? Before that, how is Evan doing?" "Much better, thanks. Sam, I'm here with the family practice residents, and a question came up. Can I put you on speakerphone?" "Sure, no problem. What's the question?"

Ron pushed the speaker button and put the handset down. "We have a question about allergy shots for poison ivy. Do you do them?"

"Yeah, frequently." Ron looked at Sailor and the residents, and they were grinning at him. The look said it all—"You're not as smart as you think you are."

Ron had to think fast. "How well do they work? I was under the impression that hyposensitization didn't work for skin allergies."

"It doesn't. You are correct." He had a little chuckle in his voice. The look of the residents' faces had changed.

"Then why do you do them?"

"Because patients want them." The response nearly blew Ron away. He didn't know what else to say.

"Well, thanks, Sam. I appreciate you taking my call during office hours."

"No problem. Anytime I can be of help with the residents, feel free to call." He hung up.

Ron switched off the phone and looked at Sailor and then the residents. He chose his words carefully. "Need I say more?" A few shook their heads. It was a verification of what he had tried to instill any number of times.

As a physician, you often had a choice: do the right thing or do things to make money. It would be how one's reputation was made.

CHAPTER TWENTY

Fairtown's radiology department didn't have a CT scanner, much less an MRI machine, a device that was just now making an entry into clinical medicine. Ron had joined his neighbor who had made a significant fortune in medical equipment and was now establishing MRI centers. Ron had invested some money with him in the endeavor. During that time, he had watched and learned how to establish and fund what were called limited partnerships. It was a way to finance the million-dollar MRI devices.

It was a simple concept. A few doctors, up to thirty-five, would invest or, more appropriately, sign a note for around thirty thousand dollars. And then while the equipment generated revenue, it would pay off the note and provide a profit. It was a way to get the expensive equipment into the hospitals.

The MRI manufacturers were only too eager to sell their products. They would even "cook the books" enough to provide excess on the lease note for what they called start-up money. Ron had watched as his business friend was able to pocket over a hundred thousand dollars from the lease money. It was essentially a commission for getting the lease, a very lucrative item for the manufacturer or the bank.

Every three months, the entire medical staff met for a general meeting to discuss hospital business. They were generally boring and often rehashed the items that had been discussed in the executive meetings. Tonight it was a surprise when Bart Freeman, the new head of the radiology department, got up to speak. Bart had finally supplanted Tom Consenti as chief of the department.

Consenti had turned seventy and wanted to work part-time. That satisfied all parties concerned.

Freeman started, "Guys, ever since I took over, and even before that, many of you have asked why we don't have a CT at Fairtown. I have discussed this with Bill a few times, and it obviously comes down to money. "We kicked around a number of ideas, but the funds just aren't there.

A million dollars is a lot for this sized hospital to absorb. Right, Bill?" He nodded in Williams's direction. Williams indicated that he was correct with a slight nod of his head.

"Wonder where this is going?" Ron turned and whispered to Steve.

He was met with a shrug of the shoulders.

Freeman continued, "So we came up with an idea. We felt that the staff should chip in and buy the CT . . ."

Before he could continue, there were multiple voices talking. It did not sound like they were taking the idea.

"Wait a minute!" Sam Wilton, an internist on staff for the past three years, was standing and posing the question. "You, the radiologists, who make more money than all of us, want us to buy a machine so that you can make more money? Is that what I'm hearing?" He remained standing. "Well, I'm not certain that you should look at it that way," Freeman weakly replied.

"How should we look at it?" a chorus returned.

"Look, you guys need this and have been pretty insistent that we get one. I can't tell you what a pain it is to ship all the patients by ambulance to Oceanside for CT scans. We need one, and this looked like the only way we can afford one. Any other comments?"

There were a number of the staff commenting, but Ron realized that none of them knew what they were saying. At a lull in the discussion and with nothing resolved, he raised his hand.

"Ron, you have something to add?" Freeman looked exasperated.

Ron rose from his chair and gathered his thoughts. "Some of you know that I have been working with a group that is establishing MRI centers in New York and Texas. These are some very smart people, and the way they are funding these centers is very creative and very legitimate. Instead of donating your money, I can show you how to get a CT tomorrow and make some thirty or so of you some money. They are called limited partnerships and meet IRS and ethical muster. You don't even need to put up cash. Signing a promissory note is all that is required, and the proceeds will pay off the note. Initially, you will get a nice tax credit and some depreciation.

"So if any of you are interested, let me know, and we can get started on having a CT or even, I might add, a state-of-the-art MRI." Ron sat down. There was a buzz in the room. A couple of the docs looked at him and indicated they wanted to talk.

Bart Freeman looked at Bill Williams. "What about that idea, Bill?" Williams slowly got to his feet and glanced at Campbell. He looked very annoyed. "Well, he may have something there, but I don't think it's a good idea for the hospital. He can't get the lease rates that the hospital can." Ron looked at him in stunned silence. What Williams just said was that the hospital was going to get a CT on lease and that the whole idea of the doctors donating the money was just to keep the account off the hospital books. Williams was maneuvering to get the lease commission.

On a million-dollar lease, it could come to almost fifty thousand. Ron had just pushed him to get started.

"Let's you and I get together about this tomorrow, Bart." Williams terminated the discussion.

A few more items were brought up, but they were just housekeeping. The meeting was adjourned. Quickly a few doctors gathered around Ron to question him on his idea. He patiently went through the details, but he knew the idea was moot.

Three days later, Ron was deep in the bowels of the hospital, standing in a darkened room and looking at films on the view box.

"Need any help?" Bart Freeman was peering over his shoulder. He always tried to be helpful and was a good radiologist.

"Well, since you're here, I was wondering what you saw in this chest film. I read the report but wanted to see it myself."

Freeman stepped up to the view box and, with a pen, showed Ron what he had seen. Ron still had difficulty making it out. "The finest shadows from shadowland," Ron said. It was an old expression.

"What we need to follow up is a CT." It came with a small laugh from Freeman.

"Yes, I know. You put that on the report. But since you brought that up, have you and Williams made a decision on the funding, or do I try to rustle up investors?"

"No, you don't have to do anything. Williams told me to meet with GE and Siemens, get the best machine, and order it."

"It's only been three days, but what did you find out?"

"I ordered a third-generation CT from GE this morning." There was a big grin on his face. "We will start to have construction beginning on the room across the hall. I figure four to six weeks."

"Congratulations. I hope that I didn't disturb anything?" He knew that he had expedited the affair, but he wanted to be tactful. Perhaps he was learning in his old age.

"Not at all, you really got the ball rolling."

Six weeks later, Fairtown had a CT. It happened just as other hospitals were installing MRI machines.

During that time, Ron had other things on his mind. One evening while Barbara was finishing cooking dinner, she casually said, "I saw Bob Garth today." It seemed innocuous.

"Oh, really? Was it for your annual Pap smear?" He was staring at the sports page.

"No, I've been having some problems."

The comment caused Campbell to turn from the paper and his martini. "What kind of problems? You didn't say anything to me about a problem." "Oh, Ron, I didn't want to alarm you, but you've been so wrapped up in cases and hospital business I thought that I should take care of it myself." "Well, what kind of problems?" Ron, like any other human, often thought of the worst.

"It's nothing too serious. In case you hadn't noticed, I've been having very heavy periods for five to six days at a time. Bob examined me and did an ultrasound in the office. He said I have a couple of very large fibroids. My blood count is down, and he started me on iron. That's why he said I was feeling so tired."

"What was your blood count?"

"He mentioned it was just under ten."

"That's your hemoglobin level. It should be twelve to fourteen. What else did he say?"

"He thought I should have a partial hysterectomy."

"Oh shit, that means surgery and anesthesia. I know that he's a pretty well-trained gynecologist, but those guys aren't the best surgeons. And no matter, if things go well, they aren't very well equipped for post-op problems."

"Well, what choice do I have? I can't very well go somewhere else." "Why not?" It was emphatic.

"Because, idiot, how would it look? You convince all your patients to go to Fairtown, and you don't want your wife to go there?"

"Did he book you for surgery?"

"No, I told him that I wanted to talk it over with you. Do you have any other ideas?"

"Maybe I'll talk to Steve about it. I'd be happier if he did the surgery." "Ron, I know you think the world of his surgical skills, but has he ever done a hysterectomy?"

"Dunno, but hysterectomies for benign diseases aren't that hard. I've scrubbed in on a few." Actually, just two, but "a few" sounded better.

"Do what you want, but I don't want to put it off too long. I'm tired of the damn things. After four kids, I don't need or want a uterus. He said he thought that he'll save the ovaries. It won't change things." She cocked an eye at him. He got her meaning.

The following day, Ron related Barbara's story to Steve over coffee in the hospital coffee shop.

"Have you ever done hysterectomies?" Ron asked.

"I did a bunch during my residency when I rotated through gyn. They're not hard if it isn't stage three or four cancer. I did two for some doctors' wives in Philadelphia. Any reason you're asking?"

"Steve, I like Bob, but I'm really uncertain that he knows how to handle post-op complications. And as we have said before, if someone is going to have a complication, it's a doctor or his family. I know he'd be pissed, but do you think you could do her surgery?"

"I'd love too. But I can't." "Really? Why?"

"Just before the hospital opened, the two gyn guys who were going to be on staff along with Carl and I made an agreement that the general surgeons wouldn't do gyn surgery and the gyn guys wouldn't do breast work. So far everyone has stayed to that."

"I never knew that. Was that the same meeting where you decided that docs like me couldn't scrub in?"

"Yeah, I think so."

"How did that come up?"

Steve looked at him for a moment, gathering his thoughts. "It initially was made for legal reasons. It could seem like fee splitting. Say you send me a case and you scrub in and then bill the insurance or patient. But the real reason was that although state law requires two in the OR, the other guys wanted it so that more money goes to the surgical or gyn group. Sorry, I know how much you like surgery." He finished with a shrug of the shoulders.

Later that evening, Ron told Barbara to have Bob Garth book her surgery. Any surgical procedures that his family had to undergo caused him to have anxiety.

CHAPTER TWENTY-ONE

"What do you know about the Millhouse girl?" Ron was so distraught that he could only spit out a few words. It was the day after the little girl's death, and Ron was at Oceanside to manage the family practice clinic for the residents. The same three—Sailor, Zowicki, and Thomas—were in Sailor's office. In retrospect, Ron realized that they were there to hear what he had to say about Fairtown.

"She came in about two this morning. She was already dead, but the guys in the ER tried to revive her. According to them, she probably expired ten, fifteen minutes earlier." Sailor was quietly explaining the situation.

"Did one of her parents come in the ambulance with her?"

"The mother. She knew that her daughter was dead when she got here, but you know how they think we can revive them. The father was following in the family car."

"What did they say after they pronounced her?" Ron was just clutching at straws.

"From what the pediatric resident in the ER said, they kept asking why Hernandez didn't come in to see her."

"The resident said that Hernandez didn't have privileges at Oceanside. He didn't realize that the parents were talking about Fairtown. They couldn't believe that their ten-year-old had died from asthma even though they had gotten her to the hospital. Children don't die from that in hospitals."

"Did anyone try to intubate the child or do a tracheotomy?" Ron knew the answer but had to ask. His question was responded with a collective shake of the heads.

Ron turned away from the three. He was attempting to regain his composure. It was something he had trained himself to do during the time he had treated the severely wounded soldiers and marines he had seen in the naval hospitals, who had just returned from the battlefields of Vietnam. Finally, not being able to control himself, he slowly looked at the three doctors. "The parents were patients of mine. They called my office to see me tonight. But let me tell you three—you are complicit in this death." "What?" It came from all three at the same time.

"This was the same thing that happened a few months ago. I begged you to write a letter to the Fairtown board. But you just laughed it off.   It seemed like a joke. And even though you knew, from not just me but others, what kind of shit was going on, you could care less. Now you can carry this with you. Academics without balls." He stomped out of the office and went to the clinic across the street.

That evening after he finished office hours, Arlene and Don Millhouse sat on the sofa in his consultation office. They slowly and tearfully reiterated what had happened two nights before.

"Sherry had severe asthma since she was small. She was in the hospital twice in the city before we moved out here. We thought that she would be better off seeing a pediatrician, and since Hernandez was the only board- certified pediatrician, we took her there." Arlene was trying to nicely explain why Ron wasn't her doctor.

"She started with an attack early in the morning, and we used the inhalers and the nebulizer. I called the office, and they said that Hernandez was very busy and would have difficulty seeing her."

"Did they tell you not to come in?" Ron was probing.

"Not in so many words. But they told me to call back later. And I did around three. She had broken a bit with our treatments but was still very tight. I wanted to know what to do."

"And?" It was all he could reply.

"They put me on hold, and when she came back on, she said that the doctor told her to tell me to try the nebulizer again. I didn't think I should use it so soon after her last treatment. But I did. It seemed to help for maybe an hour."

"Did Hernandez ever speak with you?"

"No. In fact, I called again just before five and pushed to speak to him.

They said he had left the office but they would page him." "Did they?"

"Who knows? He never called." She said it with a shrug of the shoulders.

"When did you decide to take her to the hospital?"

"About nine. She seemed to be getting worse. So we asked the neighbor to watch our seven-year-old son, and we got there before ten."

"Were they busy?" Ron was attempting to find out how soon they evaluated the child and treated her.

"Oh, the nurses were great. They took her right in and called the ER doctor. He saw her pretty quickly."

"Who was the doctor?"

"Karl Evens. Why?" This was from Don Millhouse.

Ron recognized the tone. He had to be careful. This was a minefield as he was certain that a malpractice case was coming. He didn't want to be quoted. But Evens was a real jerk, and Ron had some responsibility in hiring him.

He and Steve and two others had volunteered to set up the ER medical staff when the hospital opened. Evens was the first non–staff member that they had hired to be an employee. He was the only one that had applied.

"Just wondering how the events played out. Go on." He was looking at Arlene.

"They gave her another inhalation treatment and a couple of shots. I think one was cortisone."

"Did she get any relief from them?"

"Maybe a bit. But I kept asking when Dr. Hernandez was coming in." "What did they say?"

"They said that they called his service to have him paged. But when I asked again, they tried his home, and his wife said that he wasn't there."

"This was what time?" "About eleven, eleven thirty."

Ron was wondering what Hernandez was doing out at that time on a Monday night without his wife. "Then what happened?"

"They put her on oxygen and sent her to a room in pediatrics."

This was dumb and dumber. There wasn't any house staff in the hospital, and even the family practice residents weren't scheduled to work that night. Ron had checked. "Did anyone else see her?" He was alluding to doctors.

"I guess around one. An anesthesiologist came down and listened to her chest."

"Was it a man or a woman?" He wondered if it was Steinshaft.

"A man who talked like he had a wheeze." Don was almost smiling. "He said that he would talk to Hernandez and came back a little later and said that he had, but I'm wondering if no one else could find him, how did he?"

"What did he say?"

"He told us that Hernandez had said to transport her to Oceanside by ambulance as they had a pediatric ICU. So the nurses called the ambulance service, and when they got there, they put her on a stretcher and transported her."

"Before you go any further, did they ever take a blood oxygen level when she was in pediatrics?"

"Not that I know of," Don replied.

Ron couldn't help himself and shook his head.

"She died before we were halfway there." Arlene started to sob, and then Ron suddenly broke up and cried. He came around his desk and put his arms around her, and the three silently wept.

He finally let go, wiping his eyes on his sleeve like a little kid. "Is there anything I can do? There's nothing meaningful that I can say."

"I don't know of anything right now. Do you think that I should contact an attorney?" Don said quietly.

"I would give it a few days. Make that decision later." "Do you think we have a case?"

Ron didn't want to stir the pot, but he had to be honest. "Probably a good one," he said quietly.

CHAPTER TWENTY-TWO

Mario Hernandez never did make it back to Fairtown Hospital. Three days after the death of the Millhouse child, Hernandez checked into Oceanside Hospital with what he claimed was chest pain. Four days later, he checked out and disappeared. Also leaving her job at Fairtown was Maria Tern. Ron wasn't privy to the details, but it soon was common knowledge that the two had fled town for what initially was Louisiana.

The irony of the situation was brought home to Campbell when Hernandez's wife showed up at his office with one of their children. It was awkward for both as she apparently had been left in difficult straits with eight children who were now on Medicaid and the house up for sale. The situation became more bizarre a year later when an old-time patient of Ron's married Tern's husband, who was left with five young kids. Thirteen certainly seemed unlucky.

"So are they going to file a case?" Steve asked Ron after he had briefly stated that he had met with the Millhouses.

"Not certain. But more importantly, I've had two patients, one with a hernia and the other who had gallstones. When I suggested that they see you, the first thing out of their mouth was 'Where does he operate out of?' When I told them Fairtown, each basically said 'No way' and said they'd find another surgeon."

Ron heard a sigh. "Me too. I had a guy in who needed a colon resection and asked if I was on staff at Oceanside. I said no. He thanked me and left the office. I checked with Williams this morning, and the occupancy rate is down to 46 percent. He's bemoaning the fact that they don't know how to keep running the place while losing so much money."

"Oh well, I can't be gloating. But we tried to tell them, or at least I did, about the problems. I never told you how many stories the residents told me about the care by some of the docs. But Bill just liked to keep the pot stirred. Why try to improve care when your job could be on the line?" Six weeks later, the newspaper reported that the Millhouses had retained a lawyer, and he stated to the press that he was going to file a malpractice case against both Hernandez and the hospital. Ron thought the choice of the attorney was puzzling. He was young, had his office in Fairtown, and was associated with some questionable groups. His practice seemed geared to personal injury and not a big-time malpractice case.

The hospital remained half empty, and the almost daily reporting on various aspects of the case kept the story on the front page. Rumors were rife. Hernandez had committed suicide. He was coming back to resume his practice. He was practicing without a license. All unsubstantiated and eventually proven not true.

It seemed like the case would never get to court, which would eventually take it off the front page. But then after almost nine months, the bombshell hit. The family had settled the case. According to lawyers quoted in the newspaper, two things mitigated against going to trial. The first was that since it was not a criminal case and the defendant, Hernandez, was out of state and wouldn't agree to testify, his malpractice insurance wasn't obligated to be responsible.

The second point was due to some arcane state ruling that said the parents did not suffer economic damages since the child did not provide anything in the way of money. The only thing that the family—or more appropriately, the brother and sister—received was a modest settlement from Fairtown's insurance carrier as matter of almost goodwill.

The death of a child resulted in that no one was found to be responsible. Ron was heartsick. Multiple people, doctors mostly, all had a hand in the eventual outcome. No one ever seemed contrite. "It happens sometimes" seemed to be the consensus.

Hernandez was culpable in not coming to see the child when she was admitted; the administrator was more interested in his bottom line than hiring house staff. The entire staff was negligent in allowing a doctor like Steinshaft to remain on staff, and the nabobs of Oceanside were culpable in not even attempting to bring the problem up with the medical board and the board of trustees at Fairtown.

Six weeks after the legal case was settled, Barbara was admitted to Fairtown for her surgery.

EPILOGUE

I suspect some readers are wondering what happened to all the characters in the book some fifty years later.

Ron and Barbara Campbell are still married after more than fifty years. Ron sold his practice and became director of sports medicine at a major university. Subsequently, they moved to Florida where Ron donates his time seeing patients in a free clinic. Barbara didn't die after all. Ron now writes books.

Steven English finished doing surgery after twenty years and went into forensic medicine.

John Sailor couldn't save his residency program, and it was closed at Oceanside. The residents that hadn't finished were forced to find other programs to complete their training.

Steinshaft left Fairtown after almost twenty years. No one knows if he is still alive.

Teddy Cohen retired and was soon divorced from his wife of thirty years.

Carl Riggs retired to Florida and became a stockbroker prior to his death.

Bill Williams is alive. He left hospital management and went into real estate sales.

Mario Hernandez died about ten years after leaving Fairtown. He had married Maria Tern, causing her ex-husband to sue for divorce and bigamy as she hadn't divorced him. She, however, returned to Fairtown and moved in with Baken. He died in 2014.

William Stonebreaker died in Georgia at the age of sixty-two. His father was still alive.

Ron Gillip was asked to leave the staff of Oceanside because of unnecessary surgery. He joined the US Navy as a medical officer and became chief of cardiothoracic surgery at Bethesda Naval Hospital. Subsequent to four or five deaths secondary to surgery, he was investigated. It was found that he had falsified his application and was blind in one eye. He was sentenced to five years in the brig but was subsequently released after an appeal. He died not long after.

Stephen Grotski and the wife of the slain brother returned to Fairtown almost five years after the trial in order to file a lawsuit against the Kawasaki motorcycle company for death by vehicle. They lost. Interestingly, the case was cited by law books as an example of mercy killing.

Jack Mazzola lost his license to practice medicine when he was sixty- three for sexually molesting a patient. He died five years later.